DEATH BAKES A PECAN PIE

This Large Print Book carries the
Seal of Approval of N.A.V.H.

A FRESH-BAKED MYSTERY

DEATH BAKES A PECAN PIE

LIVIA J. WASHBURN

WHEELER PUBLISHING
A part of Gale, a Cengage Company

Farmington Hills, Mich • San Francisco • New York • Waterville, Maine
Meriden, Conn • Mason, Ohio • Chicago

Copyright © 2018 by Livia J. Washburn.
Wheeler Publishing, a part of Gale, a Cengage Company.

ALL RIGHTS RESERVED
Wheeler Publishing Large Print Cozy Mystery.
The text of this Large Print edition is unabridged.
Other aspects of the book may vary from the original edition.
Set in 16 pt. Plantin.

LIBRARY OF CONGRESS CIP DATA ON FILE.
CATALOGUING IN PUBLICATION FOR THIS BOOK
IS AVAILABLE FROM THE LIBRARY OF CONGRESS

ISBN-13: 978-1-4328-6234-3 (softcover)

Published in 2019 by arrangement with Livia J. Washburn

Printed in the United States of America
3 4 5 6 7   23 22 21 20 19

Dedicated to my husband, James, and my daughters, Joanna and Shayna, for always being willing to read a passage or taste a pie.

CHAPTER 1

"I swear, it's just like lookin' in a mirror, isn't it?" Sam Fletcher said as he peered over Phyllis Newsom's shoulder at the image displayed on the monitor. "She's the spittin' image of you."

Phyllis was sitting in her comfortable office chair in front of the desk with the computer and monitor on it. She turned the chair a little and looked over her shoulder at Sam.

"I think you need glasses," she told him. "That's a Hollywood glamour girl. She doesn't look anything like me."

"My eyes are just fine," Sam insisted.

"And she's a lot younger than me."

"Three years," Sam said. "Accordin' to IMDb. That's not much."

They were in the living room of the big old two-story house on a tree-shaded side street in Weatherford, Texas, a few blocks from the downtown courthouse square.

Phyllis had lived in this house for more decades than she liked to think about . . . well, actually, that wasn't true, she often realized. Thinking about how long she had made her home here usually gave her a real sense of continuity and serenity in her life.

For the past decade or so, since her husband Kenny had passed away, she had shared the house with several other retired teachers. Sam had been something of a latecomer in that group, but even though he was the only man, he fit in quite well. The other two boarders — although "boarders" was hardly the word to use; they were family now, like Sam — were Carolyn Wilbarger and Eve Turner, and it was because of Eve that Phyllis and Sam were looking at the photograph of Melissa Keller on the computer monitor right now.

Phyllis turned her attention back to the screen and went on, "Honestly, it had been so long I didn't think the movie would ever get made."

"Just a couple of years," Sam said. "Accordin' to Eve, that's not long at all for a project to be stuck in development hell."

"Development hell?"

"That's what they call it in Hollywood. They've got to get all the right folks attached to the project before they go ahead.

8

They need to have just the right producer and director, and the script has to be good, and of course they need the right actress to play the beautiful leadin' lady."

Sam waved a hand toward the image of Melissa Keller as if to prove his point.

"Well, I have to admit, I *am* sort of looking forward to meeting her," Phyllis said. "And everyone else, of course. I can't believe that a bunch of Hollywood movie stars and bigwigs are going to be right here in my house!"

She had never dreamed that anybody would write a book based on her, either, but it had happened. Loosely based, as Eve put it, but Phyllis had read the darned thing and as far as she could see, it was pretty close.

Through a series of unfortunate occurrences, Phyllis had found herself involved in a number of murder cases, and because of the observational and reasoning abilities she had developed over the years as a teacher — you had to be pretty sharp to keep up with those kids! — she had been able to put her finger on the killer in each case. As if that hadn't brought her enough unwanted notoriety already, her old friend and housemate Eve Turner had gone and written that novel, selling it to a publisher and then turning around and selling the movie rights to a Hollywood producer! That turn of events had been even more unexpected than the ones that had Phyllis, usually ably assisted by Sam, chasing killers.

But as she had just mentioned to him, after things had dragged on for a while, she had just assumed that nothing would ever come of the movie deal. She knew that a lot more such projects got talked about than ever got made.

All that had changed a few weeks earlier when the cast and crew of *Fresh Baked Death* had descended on Austin, the state capital, which was also the center of the film business in Texas. A lot of movies and TV shows had been made there, and as Eve had explained to her friends, most of the filming for this movie would take place there as well.

"They're using a house down there to substitute for this one," Eve had said. "From the pictures I've seen, it looks . . . sort of the same. Close enough, anyway. But things about it make it a lot easier to shoot there than it would be here. The same is true for most of the other locations. They'll just make Austin and the suburbs around it look like Weatherford and Parker County."

"That's fine with me," Carolyn had commented. "You know what they say: 'Keep

Austin weird.' So all those weirdos from Hollywood ought to fit in just fine down there. Better than they would up here, that's for sure."

"But they *are* coming to Weatherford to do some location shooting," Eve had pointed out. "They need to get some footage of the park for the Harvest Festival."

The murder in Eve's book was based on one that had actually taken place at Weatherford's annual Harvest Festival, held every November shortly before Thanksgiving at Holland Lake Park, a picturesque park on the south side of town. The festival was coming up again soon. Volunteers had already started putting up decorations on the old stone and log buildings spread out along one side of the lake.

"Hold on a minute," Carolyn had said. "Who in the world gave them permission to do that?"

"The city. Mr. Sammons, the producer, made the arrangements and got all the proper permits. With the understanding that the production company will make a sizable donation to the food pantry."

"Oh." That had mollified Carolyn, at least to a certain extent. The festival was one of her pet projects, since its real purpose was to provide food and other necessities of life for the homeless and disadvantaged families in the county. Admission to the festival consisted of a bag of canned food, but the project certainly could use financial donations, as well. Anything that would help feed those who needed it. Carolyn had gone hungry as a child. She didn't want that to happen to anyone else if she could do something about it.

"I suppose that's all right," she had continued as the four friends sat around the kitchen table. "As long as they don't interfere too much in the festival."

"They're planning to be here early enough to do all their shooting the day before the actual festival." At that point, Eve had turned to Phyllis and said, "They'd all really like to meet you. And everyone else, of course."

Phyllis's eyebrows had gone up. "Me? Us? Why do they want to meet us?"

"To help with their performances, of course. They're dedicated artists. And very nice people."

"Actors and actresses?" That comment came from Carolyn in a voice that dripped with caustic skepticism.

"I think the actresses like to be called actors now, too. And why wouldn't they be nice?"

12

"They're from Hollywood. They're all degenerates."

"You don't know that —" Eve began with a little heat coming into her voice.

"I'm sure they're like everybody else," Phyllis said, trying to inject a note of reasonableness into the conversation. "Some nice, some maybe not so nice. But there's no reason we can't all be polite to each other." She paused, then added, "In fact, why don't you invite them all here, Eve, and we'll have a dinner party for them, maybe the night before they do their filming?"

This time it was Sam's shaggy eyebrows that had gone up in surprise, and Carolyn looked almost as shocked.

"A whole crew of . . . of . . ." Carolyn couldn't come up with the word she wanted, which was probably just as well.

"Well . . . maybe not the whole crew," Phyllis had said. "I'm not sure how many people are involved in making a movie —"

"A lot," Eve said.

"But the main actors could come, certainly, if they wanted to, and maybe the producer and director."

"And the screenwriters," Eve said. "I actually know them better than anyone else. We traded quite a few emails while they were working on the script. A very nice couple.

13

Husband and wife working together, you don't see that much in Hollywood anymore."

"That's because nobody stays married more than a week," Carolyn said.

"We'll invite them, too, of course," Phyllis said. "Are they even part of the filming? I thought writers, well, just sat in a room somewhere and typed and didn't have anything to do with it anymore once their part was done."

"The director likes to have them on the set and locations, in case the script needs to be revised. From what I hear, Mr. Fremont is quite the perfectionist. He doesn't want a word of dialogue out of place or not just right."

"Lawrence Fremont?" Sam had said. "He's the one helmin' the pic?" He spread his hands as the others turned to look at him. "Hey, I've been readin' some of those movie news websites since Eve sold the rights to her book. I know the lingo. Some of it, anyway."

"Yes, Lawrence Fremont is the director."

"He's good. No John Ford or Howard Hawks, mind you, but good."

"It's settled, then," Phyllis had said. "We'll have them here for dinner, assuming, of course, that any of them want to come."

"I'm sure they will."

Since then, Phyllis had given considerable thought to what she would prepare for the meal. Hollywood people were probably used to having fancy food, but although she had been known to whip up a few exotic dishes now and then, Phyllis wasn't exactly what anybody would call fancy when it came to her cooking.

One thing she knew right away: she would be baking pecan pies. The Harvest Festival always featured a pie contest, and this would be a good chance to try out the recipe she intended to use. She didn't know if anyone from Hollywood would appreciate a good old-fashioned Texas pecan pie . . . but she would find out.

All along, Eve had been sharing the casting news as actors were picked for each role. Phyllis didn't like to think that she was particularly vain, but she was . . . interested . . . in finding out who was going to play Peggy Nelson, the character Eve had based on her. Everyone had a different name in the book, of course. Eve hadn't wanted to use their real names, and she had changed a few details about them "for dramatic purposes", as she put it.

Melissa Keller, the actress playing Peggy, was familiar to Phyllis from a number of movies and from roles in a couple of long-running TV sitcoms that had earned her a few Supporting Actress Emmy nominations. Phyllis thought she looked too young and glamorous to be playing a role that was basically *her,* because she certainly wasn't young and glamorous, but she trusted Sam when it came to pop culture, so now as she turned off the monitor she said, "I suppose that if she's only three years younger than me, they can make her look old enough. They're wizards at such things in the movie business, after all."

Sam put his hands on her shoulders as he stood behind her and said, "Maybe, but they can never make her as pretty as you."

She reached up, patted his left hand where it lay on her shoulder, and said, "You're a flatterer. Not that I mind."

"And Hollywood can't make her as smart as you, either."

"But you're still looking forward to meeting her, aren't you?"

Sam smiled and said, "I'd be lyin' if I said I wasn't."

CHAPTER 2

Accompanied by a clatter of footsteps coming down the stairs, Veronica Ericson called, "Are they here yet?"

"You would have heard the doorbell if they'd showed up already," Sam told his granddaughter as she came into the living room.

Ronnie had been staying with them for a while, after some trouble involving her and a boy she had followed to Texas from her home in Pennsylvania. Sam's daughter Vanessa and her husband Phil had been less than enthusiastic about allowing their only child to continue living more than 1500 miles away, but eventually they had agreed. Ronnie was in her senior year of high school now, and she wanted to finish here in Weatherford.

Having a blue-haired teenager in the house had livened things up, that was for sure, but Phyllis didn't mind. Actually, she

found it sort of amusing that people sometimes referred to "blue-haired old ladies",
but out of her, Carolyn, and Eve, none of
them had even remotely blue hair. Ronnie's
hair, of course, was a much brighter shade
than the stereotypical one. It was beginning
to fade back to its natural blonde, however,
and so far she showed no signs of dyeing it
again.

She came into the dining room followed
by Buck, the rescue Dalmatian Sam had
adopted a few years earlier. Ronnie and
Buck had become good friends, especially
now that Raven, the black cat Phyllis had
been taking care of for some friends, had
gone back to her own home.

"Wow, the good china," Ronnie commented as she looked at the long dining
table that was set for fourteen people. Phyllis had had to send Sam up into the attic to
bring down the leaf for it.

Phyllis cast a skeptical look at the girl and
asked, "Do you really recognize good china
when you see it?"

That brought a laugh from Ronnie. "Well,
no. Would anybody under the age of fifty?"

"Some would," Carolyn said from the
other end of the table. "Those who care
about proper entertaining and fine dining."

"My generation's a little more laid back

than that," Ronnie said. "But honestly, the table really does look nice."

"Thank you," Phyllis said. Truthfully, she *had* broken out the best china, silver, and crystal she owned. She didn't know if the movie people would notice or appreciate that, but giving her best effort was satisfying whether they did or not.

"I'll bet you're pretty excited about gettin' to meet all those movie people," Sam said to Ronnie.

"Sure, I guess. But it's not like they're young or anything. I checked out their social media, and with most of them you can tell they're not even keeping up with it themselves, they just have some hired flunky posting for them. And most of it's just publicity stuff."

Eve came into the dining room behind Ronnie and said, "The entertainment industry runs on publicity, dear. You know what they say: There's no such thing as bad publicity."

"I've actually never heard that saying before."

"And I'm not sure I agree with it, either," Phyllis added. "I've had some publicity I would have just as soon done without."

"I hope you're not talking about anything I've done," Eve said.

"Of course not," Phyllis told her without hesitation, although at times she did wish Eve hadn't ever written that novel. Still, she couldn't begrudge her old friend such success. It wasn't just the money — Eve was fairly well-to-do — but Phyllis knew she took a lot of pride in the artistic achievement, and justifiably so.

Ronnie reached down to scratch Buck's ears and said, "Now who exactly is it that's going to be here this evening? I can't remember all of them."

"Melissa Keller," Sam said. "She's the one playin' Phyllis."

"She's playing Peggy Nelson," Eve corrected him. "They're not exactly the same."

"Well, yeah, sure. There are bound to be some differences. Take that Harkness fella, the one who's playin' me —"

"Tom Faraday is the character's name," Eve said.

"Yeah, him. He's not as ruggedly handsome as I am. I still say they should've gotten Sam Elliott."

"Maybe he's involved in some other project right now," Phyllis said. "Movie stars have conflicts like that all the time, I've heard."

Eve picked up naming the guests who were coming to dinner. "Julie Cordell is playing Catherine Whittington, and Heidi Lancaster plays Liz Garrett. They'll both be here."

"You and Carolyn, right?" Ronnie asked, wagging a finger between the two women. Carolyn rolled her eyes, but Eve nodded.

"And the producer, Alan Sammons," she went on, "the director Lawrence Fremont, and the couple who wrote the script, Jason and Deanne Wilkes."

"Why didn't they let you write it? It's based on your book, after all. You know more about it than anybody else."

With a laugh, Eve shook her head and said, "Oh, goodness, I don't know anything about how to write a movie. Of course, I suppose you could say I didn't know anything about how to write a novel, either, but at least I was an English teacher for a long time and had read and studied a great many novels. I know *something* about how they're put together. From what I've heard, writing a movie is *much* different. It's all so technical."

"Did they let you read the script?" Sam asked.

"No, I didn't get an approval clause."

"But what if they, well, ruin the book?" Ronnie said.

Sam said, "A fella once asked a writer

21

named James M. Cain how he felt about Hollywood ruinin' one of his books. He's supposed to have pointed to some shelves in his house and said, 'Hollywood didn't ruin my book. There it is, right there.' That's the way I'd feel about it, if it was me." He grinned. "And if I got a good-sized check from 'em, to boot."

"I never heard of this Cain guy, but he sounds pretty level-headed."

"Never heard of . . . What about *Double Indemnity? The Postman Always Rings Twice?*"

"Nope."

Sam was muttering something about cultural deprivation while Phyllis said, "I'm sure the people did a good job on the script or they wouldn't have been hired to write it in the first place."

"Of course, from what I've read, it's the director who's the real *auteur,*" Eve said.

"You mean author?" Carolyn asked.

"Yes, that's the literal translation, but it means something a little different in film criticism."

"That explains it. I'm not an expert in film criticism."

Eve held her hands out in front of her and said, "It's the director's *vision* that really determines what a film is like. With Lawrence Fremont, every scene, ever shot, has to be perfect, or he's not satisfied."

Sam said, "Which is why his shootin' schedules run long and his movies go over-budget."

Phyllis looked at him. "IMDb?"

"Yep. I've been studyin' up. He also has trouble gettin' along with the producers and the other studio executives, he always meddles in the editin' process, and he's either chewin' the actors out or playin' practical jokes on them."

"A jokester!" Carolyn said. "I don't like him already. I've seen enough childish pranks to last me a lifetime."

"He's a very distinguished director," Eve protested. "He was nominated for a Golden Globe once."

Phyllis said, "I'll leave the rest of you to talk about this. I need to go check on dinner."

She had settled on brisket tacos with homemade organic flour tortillas, grilled peppers and onions, sliced avocadoes, tomatoes, ranch style beans, Texas caviar, spinach pomegranate salad, tortilla chips, salsa and pecan pie. A lot of work had gone into the preparations, but most of it was already done. As a result, the various aromas drifting through the house were mouthwatering, and one of the most appetizing was the smell of fresh-baked pecan pie.

"I'll come with you," Carolyn said. "I just watch movies sometimes. I don't study them like Sam and Eve do."

As Phyllis turned toward the kitchen, she motioned for the Dalmatian to follow her and said, "Come on, Buck. It's time for you to go to the back yard, before our guests get here."

Buck looked at Sam, who said, "Go on." Satisfied with that, Buck trotted out of the dining room, following Phyllis and Carolyn.

Phyllis let him out on the back porch, where his roomy doghouse was located, then closed the door and turned to the two pies sitting on the counter. The sliced brisket was warming in the oven, but the pies had come out earlier and were cooling now.

They looked good, Phyllis thought, even if she did say so herself. The deep brown of the pecan halves, the rich, lighter brown of the filling, and the ring of perfectly crimped crust all worked together to provide an enticing visual appeal. Food had to taste good, of course, that was the most important thing, but it was even better if it was pleasing to the eye, as well. That was what elevated food from sustenance to an art form, if she wanted to be a little pretentious about it, Phyllis thought as she leaned over the counter and took a deep whiff of the aroma wafting up from the pies. The best meals engaged all the senses.

Carolyn was looking at the pies, too, and asked, "Have you thought about doing something different with the crimping to give it an original look? Perhaps a wide curving crimp rather than the pinch look."

Phyllis considered what Carolyn had said. For many years, they had been friendly rivals when it came to cooking and had competed against each other in countless recipe contests, such as the one coming up at the Harvest Festival. Carolyn never took part in that one, since she was one of the festival organizers, but Phyllis planned to enter the recipe she had used for these pecan pies. Of course, if she could tweak it a little and make it even better, she was open to doing that. She trusted Carolyn's motives completely. Even when they were competing, they were always scrupulously fair and honest and never tried to sabotage each other.

"I'm not sure what I'd do," she said. "The festival isn't until day after tomorrow, so I still have time to experiment a little."

She opened the oven to take out the

brisket. Any more time and it ran the risk of being dry.

"I hope they get here soon," she said.

The doorbell rang, as if whoever was at the front door had been waiting for that cue.

But things like that only happened in the movies, Phyllis thought as she untied the apron she wore. She took it off quickly and draped it over the back of a chair at the kitchen table. She wore a nice dress and stylish shoes — not heels, she was past the age when she was going to wear heels for anybody or any occasion — and had gotten her hair fixed earlier today. She had talked Sam into putting on a coat and tie, which was no easy feat. Carolyn looked nice as well, and Eve always had the knack of looking elegant, no matter what the occasion. Ronnie was in her usual jeans, but at least she wore a nice shirt instead of a sweatshirt.

Phyllis and Carolyn went back through to the dining room where the others were waiting. Then Phyllis led the way to the front door, stepping briskly now because she didn't believe in keeping guests waiting. She put a smile on her face and opened the door.

"Hello," she said. "Please, come in. I'm Phyllis Newsom."

"And I'm Melissa Keller," said the woman in the forefront of the group on the porch as she returned the smile and put out her hand. Phyllis took it and Melissa Keller shook her hand with a warm, friendly grip.

"What'd I tell you?" Sam said. "Like lookin' in a mirror."

CHAPTER 3

Not exactly a mirror, Phyllis told herself. Melissa Keller was several inches shorter than her, and the actress's face was slightly fuller and rounder. Her hair, although cut in a similar style to Phyllis's, was more silver than Phyllis's blend of gray and brown. Of course, she might well wear a wig while she was playing the part of Peggy Nelson. Movies could really transform a person's appearance with wigs and make-up.

But all things considered, the physical resemblance between the two of them was pretty close for movie casting. Still smiling, Phyllis stepped back and went on, "Welcome to our home. All of you, please come in."

Quite a group began to enter the foyer, bringing a touch of chilly November air with them. Phyllis recognized the actors, at least vaguely, because like Sam she had looked them up on the Internet, but the ones who worked behind the camera weren't as familiar to her.

The next person through the door behind Melissa Keller was a tall, thick-bodied man with graying dark hair that grew in tight curls against his skull. He thrust out a big hand with sausage-like fingers as he said, "I'm Alan Sammons. It's a pleasure to meet you, Mrs. Newsom."

Sammons looked like he ought to be some sort of blue-collar worker, but Phyllis knew he was actually a powerful Hollywood producer. His hand practically swallowed hers as he shook with her.

Behind Sammons came two middle-aged women, one tall and angular and a bit dour-looking, the other shorter, fluffy-haired, and pretty. The taller one introduced herself as Julie Cordell, adding, "I play Catherine Whittington."

Phyllis heard Carolyn take a sharp breath behind her. If a physical resemblance was important, then the movie's casting director hadn't done a very good job with this role. Julie Cordell didn't look anything like Carolyn, and Phyllis wasn't sure even movie magic could make that happen.

As if reading her mind, the smaller woman said, "Don't worry, dear, Julie is an exceptional actor. She'll do a fine job." She took

Phyllis's hand and pumped it enthusiastically. "I'm Heidi Lancaster." She looked around the foyer and exclaimed, "And you're Eve! Oh, I'm so glad to meet you at last. I've really enjoyed playing your part so far."

Heidi Lancaster threw her arms around Eve and hugged her, an embrace that Eve returned. They didn't really *look* that much alike, Phyllis thought, but something about their personalities meshed. Whether that was Heidi acting or something natural, she couldn't tell.

"Robert Harkness," said the man who came through the door next, and Phyllis was surprised by the accent in his voice. He definitely wasn't an American, but he was tall and rangy, like Sam. Harkness spotted him immediately and shook hands.

"Glad to meet you," Sam said. "Hope you don't mind my askin', but —"

"I'm from Australia," Harkness replied. All trace of the accent disappeared as he went on in a passable Texas drawl, "But I can play American. How's that sound?"

"Mighty good," Sam admitted.

"If you've got any pointers, though, Sam, I'd be more'n happy to hear 'em."

"Sure." As unpretentious as ever, Sam clapped a hand on the actor's shoulder and said, "Come on in the livin' room and sit down, so we can get to know each other."

That left four people outside on the porch, and the next two came in together. They were a little mismatched at first glance, the man being older, shorter, and stockier, while the woman was younger, very blond, and attractive enough to be an actress herself, although she seemed to be dressing down to de-emphasize that.

"Jason Wilkes," the man said to Phyllis. He used the index finger of his left hand to push up the pair of glasses that had slid down his nose. "And this is my wife Deanne."

"The writers," Phyllis said. "I'm very glad to meet both of you."

Eve had been chattering away with Heidi Lancaster, but she turned now and said, "Jason, Deanne, I'm so happy to meet both of you at last. I feel like we already know each other, we've talked so much on-line."

Deanne Wilkes smiled and hugged Eve. "It's good to meet you, too," she said. "You gave us such wonderful material to work with, Eve. I really hope that you're pleased with what we've done."

"I'm sure I will be. I can't wait to see the finished film."

Alan Sammons said, "Well, you'll have to

wait a while, I'm afraid, Eve. We won't be releasing it until the spring, at the earliest. I'm trying to talk the studio in hyping it as a summer blockbuster."

Phyllis didn't know all that much about the movie business, but even so, what Sammons had just said immediately struck her as a bad idea. No movie based on her and her friends could hope to compete with all those special-effects-laden superhero and science fiction and thriller movies that came out during the summer. They would just overwhelm it.

But maybe Sammons knew something she didn't — given the fact that she wasn't a successful Hollywood producer and he was, he definitely knew something she didn't — so she just smiled and didn't say anything.

Now there were just two more guests, and one of them pushed ahead of the other in a not-too-polite fashion. This man had been hanging back as if he wanted to be the last to come in, but then he must have changed his mind.

He was a fairly short man, maybe five-eight, and slender, but he carried himself with a spring in his step and a confident attitude bordering on arrogance that made him seem larger. With a close-cropped salt-and-pepper beard and deep-set eyes, he reminded Phyllis of a smaller version of Abraham Lincoln. The Lincoln of the late 1850s, perhaps, before the war had taken such a toll on him and left him haggard. As a retired American History teacher, Phyllis wasn't surprised that she would think of such a thing.

The man was dressed casually, in boots, jeans, and a denim jacket. He nodded without smiling and said, "I'm Lawrence Fremont."

"Welcome, Mr. Fremont," Phyllis said. He didn't offer to shake hands and neither did she, although she *did* smile pleasantly. "Please, come in and make yourself at home."

He nodded and moved past her, hands in his pockets now, clearly not wanting to shake with anybody. That was all right, Phyllis told herself. Some people were like that and had every right to be, she supposed.

The final guest was a man in his forties with graying hair, a brush of a mustache, and a face that reminded Phyllis a little of a friendly bulldog. He took Phyllis's hand, closed his other hand over it as well, and said in a mild voice, "Thanks so much for inviting us, Mrs. Newsom. It's not often a bunch like this has a chance to get out and associate with normal people. I'm Earl

33

Thorpe, by the way. First AD on the picture."

"AD?" Phyllis said, then recalled seeing the abbreviation somewhere in her reading about movie-making. "Oh, the assistant director."

"Yeah." Thorpe's mouth curved in a grin under the mustache. "Just a flunky, I'm afraid. I'm the only non-celebrity in the group. But Mr. Fremont said I had to come along, or else there would be an odd number of people here tonight. Even worse . . . thirteen people."

"That's true. Well, whatever the reason, Mr. Thorpe, I'm very glad you're here."

"Please, call me Earl. I'm just a guy, nobody special."

Phyllis kept smiling, but she wondered if Earl Thorpe's self-effacing manner actually covered up some resentment. Lawrence Fremont had shouldered past him pretty rudely, after all, and she supposed it might be rather intimidating working around all these high-powered Hollywood egos all the time.

But none of that was any of her business, so she just ushered Thorpe on into the foyer and closed the door behind him, then raised her voice and said, "Please, everyone, let's go in the living room and sit down for a few minutes before dinner."

The living room was a little crowded with fourteen people in it, but there were places for everyone to sit. Lawrence Fremont settled immediately in the big armchair that was Sam's usual place, but Sam was already sitting in one of the chairs near the fireplace with Robert Harkness in the one beside him as the two men talked. Melissa Keller, Julie Cordell, and Heidi Lancaster were on the sofa, Carolyn and Eve on the loveseat, and the others in the armchairs and straight-backed chairs Phyllis and Sam had arranged around the room.

The only one who wasn't sitting was Ronnie, and as she stood just inside the arched entrance from the foyer, Alan Sammons patted the arm of the chair where he sat and said, "There's room for you right here, miss."

"That's all right, thanks," Ronnie said as she headed for the one empty chair next to Phyllis.

"And who are you?" Fremont asked the girl as he steepled his fingers in front of him.

"That's my granddaughter Veronica," Sam said, taking his attention away from his conversation with Harkness for a moment.

"My Lord, would you look at the clear skin on that girl," Melissa Keller said. She laughed. "If you could sell that in Hollywood, honey, you'd be richer than everybody in this room put together."

That comment made Ronnie blush, something that was very rare.

"Nothing is more valuable than youth," Jason Wilkes said. "It's the only commodity that's always diminishing."

"Did you just write that?" his wife murmured with just the faintest hint of a dagger in the words.

"I didn't plagiarize it, if that's what you mean," Wilkes replied.

Deanne just smiled and shook her head.

Well, married couples sometimes sniped at each other, Phyllis told herself, even the happiest ones.

Heidi Lancaster said to Ronnie, "Do you live here, too, dear?"

"Yeah, I'm a senior in high school, and I want to finish it out here," Ronnie said. "My folks are in Pennsylvania."

"Is there a story that goes with that?" Fremont asked bluntly. "Something we could use in the picture?"

Eve replied before Ronnie could, saying, "No, not at all. Ronnie didn't move down here until well after the time period my book is based in. Tell me, is everything set up for the filming you'll be doing at the park tomorrow?"

Alan Sammons nodded and said, "Yeah, some of the crew members are over there now making sure everything is set up and ready to go. We'd like to get all the shots we need in one day. Isn't that right, Lawrence?"

Fremont waved a hand dismissively. "We'll see how it goes. However long it takes to get everything right, that's how long we'll shoot."

Sammons frowned a little. "They're just establishing shots."

"Every frame is important, Alan, you know that."

Phyllis had a feeling that this was a discussion the two men had had before. It might have even turned into an argument from time to time. Such things were probably common in the movie-making business, though. Weren't there always clashes between art and commerce?

Sammons said, "We put out a casting call for local extras, since we want it to look like the festival is busy. There should be a good crowd there, shouldn't there, Eve?"

"Oh, yes," Eve replied. "There's always an excellent turnout for the festival. Carolyn here is one of the organizers, you know. She's been part of it from the very first."

"Is that so?" Sammons asked as he smiled

at Carolyn. For such a burly, bear-like figure, he had a certain charm about him, Phyllis realized. Or maybe that was just a side-effect of the power and influence he wielded in his profession.

Clearly a little ill at ease among these strangers, Carolyn said, "Yes, the festival benefits a cause that's very important to me."

"Feeding the hungry," Sammons said with a nod. "I couldn't agree more. I was very happy to agree to make a donation to your local food pantry. I'm sure they do good work." He turned his head as if something had occurred to him and went on, "Veronica, are you interested in doing any acting?"

"Me?" Ronnie asked in surprise. "I'm not in drama class in school or anything like that."

"The most important thing is presence, and you have that," Sammons said.

"Hold on a minute —" Sam began.

"We want local people to show up and serve as extras tomorrow, like I said, and you should be one of them. I think the camera would love you. Lawrence might even be able to find a line of dialogue or two for you. Isn't that right, Lawrence?"

"I'd have to look at the script," Fremont said coolly. "If there's something appropriate, then maybe. But if there's not . . ."

Jason Wilkes said, "Deanne and I could write a line or two if we need to, Alan. Isn't that right?"

"Of course," Deanne agreed, but she didn't sound any more enthusiastic about the idea than Fremont did.

Sam stood up and said, "Let's not get ahead of ourselves. I don't know how Ronnie's folks would feel about her bein' in a movie, and since she's a minor —"

"I'll call them and ask them about it," Ronnie said, considerably more animated than she had been earlier. The prospect of being in a movie must have broken through her outer layer of teenage irony and detach-ment. Phyllis wasn't sure she liked the idea any more than Sam did, but on the other hand, it was probably harmless enough.

Either way, it seemed like a good time to stand up and say, "Why don't we all go into the dining room? Carolyn, if you'd give me a hand with the food . . . ?"

CHAPTER 4

To Phyllis's surprise, Julie Cordell offered to help out in the kitchen.

"Call it method acting," she said to Phyllis and Carolyn as she followed them through the dining room and into the kitchen. "I used to love to cook, but I haven't done much of it in recent years. Just too busy all the time, I guess. I want to do a good job of playing your character, though, Mrs. Wilbarger."

"Please, call me Carolyn. And as Eve would be the first to tell you, Catherine Whittington isn't really all that much like me. She's really opinionated and judgmental, you know."

"I can see how she'd come across like that, all right," Julie said. Phyllis detected a hint of being careful in her voice.

"What about Ms. Keller?" Carolyn went on. "Since she's playing Phyllis's part, maybe she'd like to —"

"I think Melissa's more interested in the mystery angle," Julie said. "I know she read the novel several times to prepare, and she read some other mystery novels, too, since this is the first time she's ever played a detective. In the past, she's always been the best friend or the mom or the mother-in-law. If you give her a chance, Phyllis, I'm sure she'll pick your brain."

"I don't know if there's anything in my brain worth picking, but that'll be fine," Phyllis said as she carefully removed the aluminum wrap covering the sliced brisket.

"Oh, everything looks and smells wonderful," Julie exclaimed as she looked at the food covering the counter and stove. "I'll give you a hand taking it into the dining room. You have to tell me all about these dishes, Carolyn."

"Well, Phyllis came up with most of the menu . . ."

"And you know as much about any of it as I do," Phyllis said as Carolyn paused. "The two of you go ahead and talk."

Julie Cordell was warmer and more friendly than she had seemed at first, Phyllis realized. It just took her a little while to relax and unbend. Well, that wasn't a complete surprise. Phyllis had read that a lot of performers were actually very shy, even

41

introverted, and had been drawn to show business as a way of breaking out of their shells. Some never did except when they were on screen or on stage or in front of a microphone. Julie might well be that sort.

She picked up the brisket and carried it into the dining room, following Carolyn and Julie as they chatted and placed the covered plates of tortillas and the grilled onions and peppers they were carrying on the table. Some of the guests were standing around talking while others had already taken places at the table. Phyllis didn't care where anyone sat and hadn't tried to make any sort of seating arrangement, so that was fine. This was as much a friendly get-together as much as it was a formal dinner party, or at least she hoped that would be the case.

After several trips to the kitchen, the food was on the table, and she was ready for everyone to sit down. "All right, if the rest of you will take your seats . . ."

Two empty chairs were together on the left side of the table. Melissa Keller started toward one of them, Robert Harkness toward the other. Then both of them stopped abruptly and looked at each other, and Phyllis saw what she had missed earlier in their eyes: a deep and abiding dislike of each other.

That reaction lasted just a second before Melissa turned to Phyllis with a smile and said, "Where are you sitting? I ought to be next to you. I have all sorts of questions for you, so I hope you'll be patient with me."

"Of course," Phyllis said. "Right over here."

The chair at the head of the table was empty, and so was the one to its left. Since this was her house, Phyllis sat at the head and Melissa sat beside her. If it had been up to Phyllis, Sam would have been at the other end of the table, but Lawrence Fremont had already settled into that seat, just as he had taken Sam's usual armchair in the living room.

That annoyed Phyllis a little, but she brushed it off. When it was just the four of them here in the house, or the five of them with Ronnie, they ate around the kitchen table. That was the real center of things in a family, so it didn't really matter what happened in the dining room. Dining rooms were for other people.

Phyllis couldn't help but think about the chilliness she had just sensed between Melissa and Harkness, though. They were playing people who cared very much for each other. Would they be able to do that if they felt such genuine hostility?

That was why they called it acting, Phyllis supposed.

The meal went well, with everyone except for Lawrence Fremont complimenting Phyllis on the food. Fremont didn't seem to be the sort to pass out very many compliments to anybody about anything, so she didn't take that badly, just chalked it up to his personality.

Julie and Carolyn continued hitting it off, Sam seemed to be enjoying talking to Robert Harkness, and Eve and Heidi might as well have been long-lost sisters reunited at last. Melissa smiled at the loud, animated conversations going on around the table and leaned over to say quietly to Phyllis, "Your little get-together is a success, I'd say."

"A get-together is exactly how I thought of it earlier," Phyllis admitted. "I wasn't sure what to expect —"

"You thought we'd all be a bunch of stuck-up Hollywood snobs. Or else we'd be sniffing lines of cocaine off your dining room table. Right?"

"I don't think I ever thought *that.*"

"Well, I can't claim that everybody in this room has always been clean and sober. Dig around in any gathering and you're going to find some skeletons, you know?" Melissa laughed. "What am I saying? Of course you know. You're the crime-busting grandma. How many murders have you solved now?"

"I . . . don't really keep track of things like that."

"Maybe you should. You might be closing in on a record." Melissa took a drink of iced tea. "This is really good. Here in Texas you drink iced tea all year 'round, right, even in the winter?"

"Why wouldn't you?" Phyllis asked.

That made Melissa laugh again. "I'm going to make a mental note of that. Now tell me . . . how in the world did you manage to catch all those killers? And don't you ever get scared, dealing with the people you must run into in that line of work?"

"I don't consider solving crimes my line of work. If I never get involved with another one the rest of my life, that would be just fine with me."

"Really?" Melissa didn't sound convinced. "You mean you wouldn't miss it? The thrill of matching wits with some cunning murderer?"

Phyllis shook her head. "It's not a thrill. Too often it's just sad and tragic, the things people are driven to do to each other."

"Well, I can't argue with that. But you still

haven't told me how you do it. Exactly how do you solve a murder?"

"You have to just . . . Oh, I don't know. You listen to what people say. You pay attention to what they do. Sometimes people will say or do something for no real reason. It's just random chance. But that's rare. Almost everything has a reason, even if people aren't aware of it most of the time. So when they do something that doesn't quite fit, there's something behind it. When they say something that isn't quite right, you have to ask yourself why."

"How can you tell it isn't right? How do you know when somebody's lying?"

"I taught American History to eighth-graders for many, many years."

"Oh, Lord," Melissa said with another smile and laugh. "It was a long time ago, but I remember eighth grade . . . I think. Is there a bigger bundle of hormones and neuroses in the world than an eighth-grader?"

"Not that I know of," Phyllis said with a smile of her own.

Melissa nodded slowly and said, "I wish I had time to just sit down and visit with you for a few days. You know, sort of soak in your wisdom."

"I'm not all that wise."

"Don't sell yourself short. But time is money, you know." Melissa's eyes rolled a little. "Just ask Alan. If he makes it through the end of this shoot without strangling Fremont, I'll be surprised."

"Really?"

"Well, no, I'm exaggerating, I guess. Alan's a big guy, but he's not violent. I'm sure he feels like it sometimes, though, the way Lawrence drags his feet and shoots take after take. And then he'll do something for a laugh that slows things down even more."

"That's an odd combination, isn't it? I mean, Mr. Fremont has a reputation as such a perfectionist, and yet he also pulls pranks on people."

Melissa shrugged and said, "He claims it relieves tension on the set or on location, and that makes the shooting go better. Who knows? He'll play some practical joke, then stop everything cold while he chews somebody out, and it can be anybody from an award-winning actor to a grip. And then he'll shoot twenty takes of a simple cutaway shot." She shook her head. "Directors. They're all crazy. But don't quote me."

"I won't, don't worry." Phyllis paused. "Is that why Mr. Sammons is here instead of back in California? To . . . keep an eye on Mr. Fremont? I would think that most producers just stay in their offices, don't they?"

"That's right." Melissa sighed. "Don't quote me on this, either, but Alan's got a lot riding on this picture. He needs a hit, but he doesn't need Fremont going 'way over budget. He's not a bad guy, so everybody's trying to do their best and keep things rolling along at a good pace. We want to bring this project in on time . . . if Lawrence Fremont will let us." She sat back in her chair. "I shouldn't be talking like this. He makes good films. In the end, I suppose that's all that really matters."

Phyllis could tell that she was talking about Lawrence Fremont with those last comments, not Alan Sammons. Phyllis looked along the table to the other end, where Fremont sat toying with his food, not really talking much to anyone. There was no chance he had heard anything Phyllis and Melissa had said. The hubbub of conversation around the table provided a certain amount of privacy.

She didn't *like* Lawrence Fremont, she realized. He just wasn't a very likable man. But from what Melissa had been saying about him, he was a complex one, and Phyllis was willing to bet that he wasn't very happy. People who were driven by something inside them, as Fremont seemed to be, often had conflicting sides of their personality, and having those sides at war with each other could be exhausting. At least, she supposed that was true.

There was something to be said for a simple life. Actually, there was much to be said for it. But some people just weren't cut out for that.

When the meal was mostly over, Phyllis stood up and said, "I hope you've all saved room for desert. I have some pecan pies in the kitchen."

Melissa got up quickly and said, "I'll help you with them."

"Thanks." Phyllis looked around the table and added, "We'll be right back."

Jason Wilkes said, "Ah, if somebody could point me in the direction of . . ."

"I'll do it," Sam said.

Phyllis and Melissa went into the kitchen, where Melissa gazed at the pies waiting on the counter and said, "Oh, my goodness, don't those look good. If I could bake worth a lick, I'd ask you for the recipe, Phyllis, but I don't think it would do any good. Boiling water is a challenge for me!"

Phyllis opened a drawer, took out a knife, and said, "Let me just go ahead and cut these and plate them before we carry them in . . ."

While she was doing that, Sam ambled into the kitchen. Phyllis glanced over at him and saw that he was frowning.

"Sam, what's wrong? You showed Mr. Wilkes where the bathroom is, didn't you?"

"Yeah. Thing is, he didn't go in there by himself."

Phyllis's eyebrows rose. "What?"

"Yeah. His wife followed him in. Brushed right past me like I wasn't there."

"Good grief. Surely they're not in there . . . I mean, they're not . . ."

"Fooling around?" Melissa asked, then shook her head. "Not those two."

"That's right," Sam said. "From what I heard through the door, I reckon it's more likely one of 'em's gonna try to kill the other one."

CHAPTER 5

Phyllis could have carried two of the pies, and Sam could have taken one with the plates, but Melissa picked up one of the plates as soon as Phyllis finished cutting the pie into slices. Phyllis cut the other two and took them into the dining room. Melissa and Sam trailed her, with Sam carrying a tall stack of dessert plates.

Along the way, she glanced down the hall at the bathroom's closed door. Jason and Deanne Wilkes weren't in the dining room, so they still had to be in the bathroom. Sam had overheard them arguing and Phyllis couldn't help wondering what the disagreement was about, but she told herself again that it was none of her business.

Of course, as Carolyn had pointed out more than once, that had never stopped her before . . .

She put a smile on her face and asked,

"Now, who'd like a cup of coffee with their pie?"

"That sounds great," Alan Sammons said. "Thanks."

A trace of the Aussie accent crept back into Robert Harkness's voice as he said, "Yes, please, that would be wonderful."

Several of the others asked for coffee. Phyllis said, "I'll go get that and then serve the pie —"

"Oh, let me do that," Melissa offered. "I couldn't bake a pie as good as these to save my life, but I can put the slices out on saucers. It'll be good practice for playing you, Phyllis."

"Peggy," Eve said. "Not Phyllis."

"Sure, that's what I meant."

As Phyllis started back to the kitchen for the coffee, she saw Jason and Deanne emerge from the bathroom. Both looked tense, even angry, but as they approached the dining room, they made obvious efforts to conceal those emotions. Phyllis knew what she had seen, though, and she trusted that Sam had been right about what he'd overheard.

She arranged cups on a tray and started pouring coffee into them. While she was doing that, Eve came into the kitchen and asked, "Do you need any help?"

"No, this isn't a problem." Phyllis paused. "You can tell me if you know what's going on between Mr. and Mrs. Wilkes, though."

Eve sighed. "You mean the argument they just had in the bathroom?"

"Does everyone know about that? Sam overheard them, but was it loud enough to hear in the dining room?"

Eve shook her head and said, "No, no, nothing like that. I don't even know if anyone else noticed. Although I suspect there's been enough tension between the two of them that the others all have an idea that *something* is going on. But I'm not sure what it is. I think they're having . . . creative differences."

"Creative differences?" Phyllis repeated. "I assumed it was over . . . well, you know . . ."

"I have no idea if either of them is cheating on the other, but I do know I'd get an email from one of them asking me a question about the book or the characters, or suggesting something that might go in the script, and then I'd hear from the other one with something totally different. After a while, I got the idea that each of them was writing their own draft of the script, and when they tried to reconcile them, it caused quite a fuss."

"And they're still arguing over a movie script, even while shooting is going on?"

"I don't know, dear. That's just how it appears to me."

Eve was usually pretty observant and had a good grasp of human nature. Anyone who had been married as many times as she had, and been through as many tragedies, had to have been exposed to a wide range of emotions. So it was entirely possible Jason and Deanne were just bickering over their writing. Phyllis had done enough writing herself, having turned out a magazine column for a while, that she knew how someone could get emotionally invested in the words they produced.

"Sam said he thought they might try to kill each other."

Eve shook her head and said, "Oh, no, it would never go that far. I'm sure of that."

"How did those two get together, anyway? They seem like a bit of an odd match."

"Deanne won some sort of screenwriting contest. She lived in Ohio and sent in her script, and when it won, it was optioned and the production company hired Jason to do a rewrite. He was already in Hollywood and had been working as a writer for a while. He'd sold several scripts and a few of them actually were produced. Deanne went out to California to get involved in the process, the two of them met . . ." Eve smiled. "Their story would have made a good movie itself. A nice little indie rom-com. Since then they've gotten married and worked on several pictures together. Whatever it is that's bothering them, I'm sure they'll put it behind them."

"Well, I hope so, for the sake of this movie." Phyllis picked up the tray with the coffee cups on it and headed back to the dining room.

Melissa was still passing out plates of pie. Jason and Deanne seemed to be on good terms again, or at least pretending to be. Sam, Robert Harkness, Alan Sammons, and Earl Thorpe were talking together at one end of the table, the seating arrangements having shifted some while Phyllis was in the kitchen. Julie Cordell and Heidi Lancaster were talking to Carolyn and Ronnie.

Lawrence Fremont still sat at the other end of the table, not talking to anyone. Melissa placed a saucer with a piece of pecan pie on it in front of him, and Phyllis went down the other side of the table to add a cup of coffee.

"Here you are, Mr. Fremont," she said. "I hope you enjoy it."

"I don't eat many sweets," Fremont said.

Sammons let out a booming laugh and said, "Don't believe him, Mrs. Newsom. The man's got a real sweet tooth. Don't you, Lawrence?"

Fremont glared a little at the producer and didn't answer. He picked up his fork, took a bite of the pie, and for the first time, Phyllis saw something that resembled a smile on his bearded face.

"This is very good," he said. "Excellent, in fact."

"Thank you," Phyllis said. She passed out the rest of the coffee while Melissa made sure everyone got a slice of pie.

Except for herself, Phyllis noted. As Melissa sat down and picked up her coffee, Phyllis asked, "You don't want any pie?"

"Oh, I want some," Melissa said, "but I can't afford the calories. I have to watch my girlish figure, you know. I can tell that you're naturally slender, but I've never been that fortunate."

"I'm sorry. Maybe I shouldn't have baked pies —"

"Oh, goodness, don't think a thing of it," Melissa said with a laugh. "Appearances are everything in Hollywood. We're used to watching what we eat and denying ourselves some of the things we really want." She shrugged. "That's probably why some of us are so self-indulgent in other things."

Phyllis wasn't sure exactly what Melissa meant by that, but she decided it was best not to probe too deeply into the subject.

Everyone complimented the pie. Phyllis thanked them graciously, then said, "This is the recipe I'm going to be entering in the contest at the actual Harvest Festival this weekend. Do any of you have any suggestions on how I might make it better?"

Sammons laughed and said, "This isn't exactly the group to ask about something like that, Mrs. Newsom. I mean, what do any of us know about baking?"

"Speak for yourself, Alan," Julie Cordell said. She was definitely more relaxed than she had been earlier in the evening. "I did quite a bit of baking in my younger years. I didn't make all that many pecan pies, but I can tell you, my crusts were very good."

Carolyn, sitting beside Julie now, nodded and said, "I've always taken pride in my pie crusts."

"See?" Julie said. "That's why I'm playing the part I am. We're more alike than you'd think by looking at us, aren't we, Carolyn?"

"It seems that way to me," Carolyn agreed.

Phyllis was a little surprised to see that Carolyn was getting along so well with somebody from Hollywood. Carolyn never warmed up quickly to strangers or outsiders, and to her someone from California — let alone Hollywood — was like a visitor from another planet. It had even taken her a while to start liking Sam, and he was Texan through and through. But Phyllis was glad to see Carolyn enjoying herself.

"So the one thing I think you could do," Julie went on to Phyllis, "would be to crimp the crust a little differently. This traditional crimp makes it look like every other pie. The pie wouldn't taste any different, but that would give it a distinctive look."

"I was just saying the same thing earlier," Carolyn exclaimed.

Julie nodded. "Like I said, we're on the same page."

"I'll certainly keep that in mind," Phyllis promised. "I thought I'd bake at least one more tomorrow. Maybe I should experiment a little."

Lawrence Fremont said, "If you come to watch us shoot tomorrow, you should bring one with you."

"You mean we're invited to the shooting?"

"Of course you are," Sammons said. "All of you. This picture wouldn't even exist without you folks. You're welcome to watch. In fact, we can put *all* of you in the movie if you want, not just Ronnie."

58

"Oh, no," Carolyn said immediately. "I wouldn't want to be on screen."

"Ronnie hasn't talked to her parents yet, either," Sam pointed out.

"But they're not going to mind," the girl said. "I'm sure of that." She turned to Sam. "Especially if you say that you're going to be there keeping an eye on everything."

"Well, I've got to admit, I've always been pretty interested in movies . . ."

"It's settled, then," Sammons said, resting his hands flat on the table. "You'll all be there, and any of you who want to be extras, that'll be fine, too."

"Maybe you'll wind up movie stars," Heidi Lancaster said.

"That'll be the day," Sam drawled with a shake of his head.

When everyone was finished with the pie, they took their coffee and went back to the living room to sit and talk for a while longer before the gathering broke up. Only one slice of pie was left, and Phyllis was about to get the plate and carry it back to the kitchen when Melissa picked it up instead.

"I'll put this away," she volunteered. "You go sit down and enjoy what's left of the evening, Phyllis. You've earned it."

Phyllis started to object, then decided not

to. Instead she nodded and said, "Thank you." She felt an instinctive liking for Melissa Keller that she hadn't expected, based on what she had looked up about the actress before meeting her. Melissa really was more down to earth than the typical Hollywood star.

Or maybe she just knew how to project that impression. When it came to actors, what was real, and what was artifice? And in the long run, did it matter?

"There's a plastic pie cover in the upper cabinet, to the right of the sink," she went on. "You can just set it over the plate."

Phyllis started toward the living room, but on the way she met Earl Thorpe, who had an empty coffee cup in his hand. The assistant director smiled and said, "Is there any left, or did we drink it all up?"

"I think there's some," Phyllis said, "but will you be able to sleep if you drink any more coffee this late, Mr. Thorpe?"

"Earl," he corrected her. "And I'm afraid I won't be sleeping for quite a while anyway. Once we get back to the hotel, I have a lot of work still to do before we shoot tomorrow. I need to go through the shot list and figure out all the blocking."

"Doesn't the director do that?"

"Some do," Thorpe said with a shrug.

"Mr. Fremont concentrates more on the performances and the script than he does on the technical details. He leaves most of that to me."

"But doesn't that make you . . . co-directors, I guess?"

Thorpe laughed, but he cast a nervous glance over his shoulder at the same time. "Don't let him hear you say that. There's only one director on a Lawrence Fremont film, no matter who does what."

"Don't worry, I won't mention it. I just like to see people get the credit that's coming to them. It's only fair."

"Fremont's going to get what's coming to him, and maybe sooner than he thinks." Thorpe grimaced. "Blast it, I shouldn't have said *that,* either."

"What are you talking about, Mr. Thorpe? I mean, Earl."

"Just forget it, okay? I should've kept my big mouth shut —"

"Something's wrong, isn't it?" Phyllis said. "Is it going to endanger the movie?"

"You could say that. Fremont . . ." Thorpe looked around to make sure no one was in earshot, then went on, "Look, I wouldn't say this if I didn't like you folks. You saw the way Alan sort of played up to Mr. Fletcher's granddaughter —"

"Yes, and I thought it was a bit unsavory, to tell you the truth. Ronnie's underage, and even if she wasn't, a man in a position of power shouldn't use that to pursue women."

"Yeah, tell that to half the guys in Hollywood these days! It's a big deal, and don't get me wrong, it should be. But Alan . . . Alan's all talk. You don't have to worry about him. He's really not a bad guy. Fremont, on the other hand . . ."

"He didn't say anything improper," Phyllis pointed out. "He didn't even seem that enthusiastic about having Ronnie in the movie."

"That's because he's got one of the other girls in the picture on the string right now, a kid named Becca Peterson. And she came to me and cried on my shoulder while we were down in Austin. Said she was going to go public on the Internet about what he's been doing. That would be likely to shut down production."

And ruin things for Eve, Phyllis thought. But on the other hand, if Fremont was taking advantage of someone, he shouldn't get away with it.

She asked Thorpe, "What are you saying, Earl? That Sam shouldn't allow Ronnie to be in the movie?"

"No, just that he needs to keep an eye on her, that's all."

"He would do that anyway. He's very protective of her."

"I'm glad to hear it." Thorpe grinned and shook his head. "Dang, I can see how you've managed to solve all those murders, Mrs. Newsom. I didn't intend to tell you any of that. I just came back here to get another cup of coffee, and instead I wind up spilling my guts."

"You were just trying to be helpful by warning me about Mr. Fremont, and I appreciate that. I'll talk to Sam, and we'll make sure that nothing improper takes place."

"I don't think it would have, anyway — like I said, Fremont's already pretty occupied, and he doesn't know a bomb's liable to go off in his face sometime soon — but it never hurts to be careful."

A step in the hall behind her made Phyllis look around. Melissa came from the kitchen, smiled, and said, "I hope you don't mind, Phyllis, but I snooped around your cabinets some. Research, you know. For getting into the character better."

"That's fine," Phyllis assured her. "There are no secrets in my cabinets!"

"Oh, secrets can pop up in places where

you never expect them," Melissa said.

Phyllis traded a quick glance with Earl Thorpe and thought that that was certainly true.

CHAPTER 6

Knowing what she knew now, Phyllis found it a little difficult not to glare at Lawrence Fremont while the entire group sat in the living room chatting and finishing their coffee. She hadn't liked him to start with, and what Earl Thorpe had told her just confirmed that initial impression.

However, being a gracious hostess was ingrained in her, and Fremont wasn't actually doing anything other than sitting there sipping coffee and making an occasional comment, so she was able to put her negative feelings for him aside and concentrate on the other people in the room.

They really were a friendly bunch, not at all what she had thought they would be like. Of course, as performers the actors were accustomed to being "on" and making people like them. That was their stock in trade, after all. And Alan Sammons, as a producer, was a deal-maker and something of a glad-hander, so he knew how to be likable, too.

The surliest person in the room, even more so than Fremont, was probably Jason Wilkes. The earlier argument with his wife had left him brooding. Deanne was still friendly enough with everybody else, but her laughter had a slightly brittle edge to it. She was keeping up appearances, but Phyllis could tell that she was upset, too.

Phyllis enjoyed talking to Melissa Keller enough that she was sorry to see the evening end, and Carolyn and Eve seemed to feel the same way about Julie Cordell and Heidi Lancaster. Sam clearly had bonded with Robert Harkness. But there was shooting to do the next day, and as Sammons said, "We have an early call in the morning, folks, so we'd better call it a night." He looked around at the others. "Nobody's sleeping in, right?"

"We'll be on time, boss, don't worry about that," Earl Thorpe said. Maybe he was sucking up a little, Phyllis wasn't sure about that, or maybe he was just being legitimately conscientious.

Everyone stood up and said their good nights. A few hugs were even exchanged. Despite enjoying the evening overall, Phyllis heaved a sigh of relief when all the guests had filed out and the front door closed behind them.

"I think that went wonderfully well, don't you?" Eve said.

Other than screenwriters fighting in the bathroom and a sexually harassing director, Phyllis thought. But she said, "It was very nice." She turned her head to look toward the dining room. "Now there's all the cleaning up to do."

"We'll help you with that," Sam said without hesitation. "Come on, Ronnie."

"Should I call Mom and Dad and ask them about being in that movie?" Ronnie said. "It's an hour later in Pennsylvania, you know."

Phyllis knew she wasn't just trying to get out of helping. Ever since Ronnie had been here, she'd been willing to pitch in with chores. So Phyllis said, "Yes, you go ahead and call them. We can take care of everything else. I'm not going to try to get all of it cleaned up tonight."

She did want to get her pie plates in the dishwasher, though, because she planned on using them early the next morning. She could put that one piece of leftover pie on a saucer.

After she, Sam, and Carolyn cleared the table and brought all the dishes to the kitchen while Eve collected the coffee cups in the living room, Phyllis lifted the pie cover and saw that the pie plate under it was empty after all. She laughed.

"What is it?" Carolyn asked.

"Now I understand why Melissa volunteered to bring this in here," Phyllis said. "She didn't eat any pie earlier because she said she was watching her figure."

Carolyn pointed a finger at Sam and admonished him, "Don't you say anything."

Sam held up his hands, palms out defensively, and gave her a wide-eyed, innocent look.

"In here by herself, though, she gave in to temptation," Phyllis went on.

"And ate that last piece of pie," Carolyn said.

Sam said, "Hey, there's a mighty good chance I would've done the same thing. There's nothin' better than holdin' a piece of good pie in your hand and eatin' it standin' up in the kitchen. I've done just that many a time."

"I don't doubt that," Carolyn said.

Sam held up a finger. "The secret is, you've got to cup your other hand under the pie, see, to catch any crumbs you might drop —"

"Yes, we get the idea."

Phyllis put both empty pie plates in the dishwasher, along with the other dishes that would fit, and started it rinsing.

Sam picked up the carafe from the coffee-maker and said, "There's just a little bit left if anybody wants it."

"I thought Mr. Thorpe was going to finish it off," Phyllis said. "He told me he still had a lot of work to do tonight to get ready for the shooting tomorrow. There must have been more than he wanted."

Sam held up the carafe and cocked an eyebrow. Carolyn shook her head and said, "Too late for me."

"Me, too," Phyllis said. "If you don't want it, Sam, just pour it down the sink."

He was doing that when Eve came in with the cups. She stacked them on the other side of the double sink, then pulled out a chair and sat down at the table.

"You know, a lot of the time I still can't believe this is happening," she said. "I mean, we had movie stars and a famous director right here in the house tonight. How is that even possible?"

Phyllis, Carolyn, and Sam sat down at the table as well, and now that the four of them were alone, the sense of camaraderie in the kitchen was strong and comforting. Phyllis was a little troubled, though, so after a moment's hesitation she said, "I know this means a lot to you, Eve."

"Well, of course it does. I mean, they're making a movie out of my book! Just writing a book was more than I ever thought I'd accomplish, let alone selling it and then having a movie made from it."

"And your accomplishment will always be every bit as remarkable and worthwhile, no matter what else happens."

"What in the world does *that* mean?" Carolyn said.

"Yeah, you sound like you're a mite worried about something," Sam added.

Eve frowned and leaned forward. "Is something wrong, dear?" she asked Phyllis. "Why would anything happen that might cause problems for the movie? That's what you're talking about, isn't it?"

"It's just that movie people are, well, undependable, aren't they?"

"No more so than anybody else. If you're concerned about the friction between Deanne and Jason, don't be. There's a shooting script that everyone has signed off on, and they're professional enough to work together and make any necessary revisions, no matter if they are having marital problems —"

"They are?" Carolyn interrupted.

70

"They were fussin' some in the bathroom earlier," Sam told her.

"Oh. I missed that. But I was enjoying talking to that Julie Cordell. I liked her a lot more than I thought I would at first."

So had Phyllis, but that wasn't really what they were talking about at the moment. Now that the subject had been broached, she knew Eve would worry if she refused to say anything else, so she said, "I could tell that Melissa and Mr. Harkness don't really like each other."

"Oh, they hate each other," Eve said. "I know that. Everybody in Hollywood knows that."

That statement made Phyllis blink. "They do?"

"Yes. I don't know what it's about, but they don't care for each other at all."

"Then how are they going to play people who *do* care for each other?" Phyllis looked across the table at Sam, and he looked back with a twinkle in his eye.

"They're professionals, like Jason and Deanne. They know how to do their jobs, regardless of any personal feelings they may have. That's a tradition that goes 'way back in Hollywood."

"Yeah, I remember readin' about some couple who were supposed to be in love on

71

screen — Fredric March and Veronica Lake, maybe — who hated each other so much they pulled all sorts of tricks to ruin each other's performances," Sam said. "I don't think Bob Harkness would do that. He struck me as a pretty decent sort of fella."

"Melissa seemed the same way to me," Phyllis admitted. "So maybe I was just worrying too much about the way they feel about each other."

Eve put her hands on the table and said, "Well, if that's all —"

"Earl Thorpe told me some things about Mr. Fremont. Things that are more serious."

Sam said, "Now that Fremont fella . . . I never could quite warm up to him."

"For once we're in complete agreement, Sam," Carolyn said.

"What's wrong with Lawrence Fremont?" Eve asked, and now she was starting to sound a little annoyed. "He's a very respected director."

"For the films he makes, maybe, but there are rumors he takes advantage of young actresses who work for him."

Sam's hands tightened on the edge of the table. "That son of a . . . and Ronnie wants to be in that movie . . . Wait a minute." He frowned. "It was Mr. Sammons who asked Ronnie if she wanted to be an extra or even have a little speakin' part. And he's the producer. Those fellas are the ones who usually get too forward with the gals, aren't they? Fremont didn't seem to care one way or the other whether Ronnie was in the movie."

"I know," Phyllis said, "but that's what Mr. Thorpe told me. I get the feeling that Mr. Sammons may be a bit, well, sleazy, but he doesn't actually *do* anything. Fremont does, though, and again according to Mr. Thorpe, he has something going on with one of the actresses working on this film. And she's talking about accusing him of inappropriate behavior, which as we all know would result in a great deal of bad publicity these days."

"A ton of it," Sam muttered.

"Would that be enough to ruin the movie?" Carolyn asked.

"I don't know," Eve said, "but it might be. It would be a terrible thing to happen." She sat back and looked distraught. "And now I'm feeling like a terrible person because I don't know what to hope for. If Mr. Fremont really has been doing something like that, then his behavior deserves to be exposed and he ought to take whatever consequences he has coming to him. The women he took advantage of deserve justice as well." She shook her head. "But couldn't it all wait until after my movie comes out?" The question was practically a wail of despair. "And that's why I feel like a terrible person, because I'm so conflicted!"

"What if that fellow Thorpe is lying?" Carolyn asked. "Maybe he made up the whole thing."

Phyllis said, "He seemed sincere enough when he told me about it. On the other hand, it *was* sort of a revelation out of the blue."

"Could be he's tryin' to stir up trouble," Sam suggested.

"Why would he do that?"

"Fremont's the director, Thorpe's the assistant director. Sometimes the number two man gets ambitious."

"And Mr. Thorpe does a lot of the work on the picture," Phyllis mused. "If he was going to spread rumors in hopes of causing trouble for Mr. Fremont, though, why tell me? I don't have anything to do with the production."

"It seems to me like an awful lot of backstage drama," Carolyn said.

"That's right," Eve said, seizing on the idea. "No production as big and complicated and expensive as a movie ever runs completely smoothly. It couldn't. I'm sure these sorts of things go on all the time, it's just that normal people like us aren't aware of them. We just go to the theaters and watch the movies and don't think about what goes into them."

"Like eatin' sausage," Sam said.

"I haven't seen a movie in a theater in fifteen years or more," Carolyn put in. "I'd rather watch them here on our own TV."

"Well, there's nothing we can do about any of those problems," Phyllis said. "The people who are actually involved with them will have to sort them out. We'll watch them shooting at the park tomorrow, and if everything goes according to schedule, they'll head back down to Austin to finish the movie. It's out of our hands, so we should just hope for the best."

"I wish I knew what that was," Eve said with a sad little smile on her face, and not for the first time in her life, Phyllis thought that she should have kept what she knew to herself.

CHAPTER 7

Phyllis was up early the next morning, before anyone else in the house. She enjoyed the peace and quiet, the little respite before the day really began. Although, with everything she had to do today, she didn't really have time for relaxing. Wearing her pajamas and robe, she opened the back door to let Buck in, and while he curled up in a corner, Phyllis got busy mixing the ingredients for another pecan pie.

Carolyn appeared a while later and poured herself a cup of the coffee Phyllis had started brewing. She carried it to the other end of the counter and looked at the pie crust dough Phyllis was gently laying into a clean pie plate from the dishwasher.

"Show me again what you were talking about on the crimping," Phyllis said.

Carolyn set the cup down and demonstrated. "Like this." Her fingers deftly pinched the dough around the plate's rim using the curve of her finger laid sideways to pinch the dough around. The result was a large crimp. Then she took a knife from the drawer and used it to etch a pattern in the dough along the rim.

"I like that," Phyllis said. "It's very distinctive."

"I saw one once where someone had taken a toothpick and actually drawn little floral designs in the edge of the crust. I'm afraid my eyes aren't good enough to do such close, intricate work."

"Mine, either," Phyllis replied with a shake of her head. She took the knife from Carolyn. "Let me give this a try, though."

They worked together in companionable fashion until the crust's rim looked satisfactory. Phyllis was eager to see what it would look like once it was baked. She reached for the bowl with the filling, poured it into the crust, scraped out the last of it with a spatula, then used it to smooth the filling before flipping the pecan halves that were upside down. She had baked so many pecan pies over the years that her movements were automatic. She didn't have to think about what she was doing as she hummed softly to herself under her breath.

"Leave the oven on, I'll put some bacon in, and then whip up some omelets," Carolyn said. She opened the refrigerator and took out the bacon, eggs, mushrooms, spinach, peppers, and a block of white cheddar cheese.

By the time Sam walked into the kitchen, the sun was up and the room was filled with delicious aromas. He stopped just inside the door, closed his eyes, and drew in a deep, appreciative breath.

"I tell you, if wakin' up in the mornin' and knowin' the Good Lord's given you another day to make use of wasn't enough of a reward by its own self, takin' a good whiff of that will sure make you give thanks. Praise the Lord and pass the silverware."

"The bacon isn't ready yet," Phyllis told him, "and the pie is going to the park for the movie people." She paused and frowned. "I should have made one for the crew, too. I wonder if there's still time . . ."

Ronnie hurried into the kitchen with an excited look on her face. It was rare to see her up this early on a day when there was no school. Classes had been dismissed early the day before, giving the students Friday off leading into fall break the next week, which included Thanksgiving.

"I just got a call from Mr. Thorpe," she said, holding up her cell phone. "He asked me for my number last night so he could let me know when to be at the park today. Shooting is supposed to start at ten o'clock, but the extras need to be there at nine."

Sam glanced at the clock on the microwave and said, "We can head over in plenty of time to get you there by then."

"I don't want to be late. They might not use me if I am."

"We won't be late," Sam assured her.

Phyllis knew from talking to him later the previous night that Vanessa and Phil, Ronnie's parents, had agreed to her being in the movie, although they had displayed some reluctance at first. The relationship between them and Ronnie was still fragile enough that they hadn't wanted to dig in their heels too much, Phyllis suspected. And honestly, no matter what gossip she had heard, with Sam there to keep an eye on things she wasn't too worried about Ronnie.

Carolyn took the pan of bacon out of the oven and said, "Give me a minute to plate all of this."

Phyllis's pecan pie was already cooling, having come out of the oven a short time earlier. She'd set out a plastic pie container to put it in when it was ready.

Eve was a notoriously late sleeper, but the prospect of watching the movie based on her book being shot had her excited enough that she rose and joined the others in the kitchen a short time later. They all sat down and ate breakfast together, something that Phyllis always enjoyed. The atmosphere in the room was even brighter and more excited than usual this morning. It was going to be a big day in Weatherford.

Phyllis had checked the weather forecast the night before, because rain would have ruined the movie company's planned shoot. Nature had cooperated, delivering a crisp, cool, clear autumn day to north central Texas, including plenty of sunshine. This was one of Phyllis's favorite times of year, although its duration was usually too short, Texas weather being in the habit of going from oppressively hot to freezing cold seemingly in the blink of an eye. A beautiful day like this was to be relished and enjoyed while it was here.

Sam and Ronnie left the house first, heading for Holland Lake Park in Sam's pickup. Phyllis, Carolyn, and Eve would come along a little later in Phyllis's Lincoln, arriving at the park closer to the time when shooting actually would begin. Carolyn was adamant that she didn't want to appear on-screen.

"I don't need any of that nonsense," she said as Phyllis was putting the pie into the plastic container. "My ego doesn't require any stroking."

"I'll take all the ego-stroking I can get," Eve countered. "I don't believe there are many writers who wouldn't."

"Yes, I imagine that's true of anyone who would make up a huge pack of lies and believe that people would actually want to read them."

Eve laughed. Phyllis knew her friend had been around Carolyn 'way too long to be offended by any of her blunt statements like that.

"That's exactly what fiction writers are," Eve declared. "Professional liars. The only profession other than politics where one can make a living at it."

Phyllis sealed down the lid on the pie container and said, "All right, I'll go get dressed, and then we'll be ready to go."

She put on jeans, a long-sleeved shirt, and a light jacket, then got the pie container from the kitchen counter as she led Carolyn and Eve out to the garage. They headed down South Main toward the park, and as she did every time she ventured in this direction, Phyllis lamented the huge increase in traffic over the past decade. Weatherford was no longer the little country town that had been her home for so long. It wasn't as congested as Fort Worth or Dallas, but someday it might get there. Of course, by that time those big cities would be even worse, and anyway, that would be after her time, Phyllis mused, so she wouldn't have to worry about it.

Holland Lake Park was located in a thickly wooded area a short distance off South Main, with a smaller road that circled the park and made a loop back to the thoroughfare. The lake was more of a pond built on a creek that ran through weedy marshes above and below the impoundment. Picnic tables could be found on both sides of the lake, but the north side was more developed, with playground equipment, restrooms, and two old, authentic log cabins that had been brought into town from out to the west in Parker County.

Those cabins had some historical significance, being two of the oldest buildings in the county, and had belonged to early pioneers. Constructed in the dogtrot style, with separate rooms on either side of a roofed, open area in the center, they had been furnished to look like that had in those olden days, with spinning wheels, antique tables and chairs, and four-poster beds with handmade quilts. The cabins weren't open to the public, but Phyllis always enjoyed peering through the windows into them.

The park held other memories that weren't so pleasant. A few years earlier, hay bales had been stacked up in one of the dogtrots so that a scarecrow could be arranged sitting on them as a decoration for that year's Harvest Festival. The scarecrow was there, all right . . . but Phyllis and Carolyn had discovered that instead of straw, inside the old clothes was the body of a murder victim!

That grim turn of events had plunged Phyllis into the middle of a complex investigation that resulted in the killer's arrest. Phyllis could take some satisfaction from that, but the initial discovery had been such a shock that she would never forget it.

When she reached the turn for the smaller road that would take them down to the park, she was surprised to see that a police car was angled across the road in such a manner that while it was possible for other cars to get past, they couldn't do so easily without stopping first. Phyllis made the turn and eased the Lincoln to a halt.

A uniformed officer walked over as Phyllis rolled the driver's window down. Her heart had started to beat faster. Were the police here because something was wrong? Sam and Ronnie had been headed here when they left the house. A pang of worry for their safety went through Phyllis.

"What in the world?" Carolyn said, sounding concerned, too.

The officer nodded to Phyllis. He didn't appear to be upset about anything, so she took that as a good sign. He said, "Morning, ma'am. The park's closed to the public today. There's a movie crew doing some filming in there."

Relief flooded through Phyllis. Of course, that made perfect sense. The movie people had a permit to shoot here and part of their arrangements with the city probably included closing the park for the day, or at least as long as the shooting was going on. They had to control who had access, so that nobody wandered into a shot and ruined it.

"We're supposed to be here," Phyllis said. "We were invited."

"You're some of the extras? They're assembling on the other side of the park, so you'll need to drive around to the other entrance and there'll be somebody there to tell you where to go."

Eve was in the back seat. She leaned forward and said, "The movie they're making is based on my novel. The producer and director and stars were at my friend's house for dinner last night. Mr. Sammons is the one who invited us to come and watch the

84

filming today."

"Oh, why didn't you say so?" the officer asked.

"She just did," Carolyn said.

To head off any hard feelings, Phyllis went on quickly, "My name is Phyllis Newsom. My friends are Eve Turner and Carolyn Wilbarger. You probably have our names on a list . . ."

"Sure, of course. I remember seeing them. You can go on in. Sorry, Miz Newsom."

"That's all right. You're just doing your job."

Phyllis smiled at the man, took her foot off the brake, and carefully drove around the police car. She followed the smaller road past some Little League baseball fields and then the park came into view.

Half a dozen good-sized trucks were parked in the asphalt-paved lot, as well as some SUVs and expensive cars. Lined up on the other side of the street were half a dozen large motor homes. Phyllis wondered if they were used as dressing rooms for the stars. She got the last available place in the lot for the Lincoln.

Flowerbeds, most with cactus growing in them, and concrete walkways divided the asphalt lot from the park itself. As Phyllis, Carolyn, and Eve got out of the car, Phyllis saw at least a hundred people milling around and talking in loud voices, as well as numerous pieces of large, unfamiliar equipment, probably lights and cameras. Moviemaking appeared to be an exercise in controlled chaos. That agreed with some of the things she had read about it. Of course, all that chaos would come to an abrupt halt whenever Lawrence Fremont called, "Action!"

Eve handed her the pie container, which had been in the back seat on the drive over. Phyllis took it and looked around, searching for a familiar face.

Before she could find one, a young man holding a clipboard hurried over to them and said, "What are you ladies doing? You're not supposed to be here —"

"Yes, they are, Chad," a booming voice said. Phyllis looked around to see Alan Sammons striding toward them. The producer went on to the young man, "These lovely ladies are with me." Then he put an arm around Eve's shoulders while he waved the other hand toward the lake and said, "Come on. I'll show you how the magic is done."

CHAPTER 8

"We don't want to take you away from your work, Mr. Sammons," Phyllis said as the producer led them along one of the concrete walks toward the lake.

"Alan, remember?" he said. "And you're not really taking me away from anything. By the time the process gets to this point, my services aren't really needed all that often. Everything is in the hands of the director, the AD, the director of photography, the grips, people like that. They know what they're doing, and somehow the system all comes together and functions. The only time they need me is if something goes wrong and somebody has to step in and referee."

"The producer isn't even on location most of the time, isn't that right?"

Sammons shrugged. "Some are more hands-on than others. In the old studio system, the director was also the producer at times. That's not as common now because everything is more compartmentalized. That's due to the unions, to a certain extent, and also to the fact that the studios don't really make movies anymore. Production companies do, and there might be half a dozen of them involved in the same picture. The big stars nearly always have their own production company, so when they agree to act in a movie, they're going to get a producer's credit, too. It's always been a big business. Lots at stake for everybody." He grinned. "Are you thinking about getting into the movie business, Phyllis?"

"Goodness, no," she said. "I just like learning about new things. That helps keep the brain sharp at my age."

Carolyn said, "I don't think you have to worry about keeping your brain sharp. Solving murders ought to take care of that just fine."

"It would be perfectly all right with me if I never had another murder to solve."

"That's what you keep saying," Carolyn replied, "but it never seems to work out that way, does it?"

Phyllis didn't have any answer for that.

Luckily she didn't have to, because Melissa Keller came up to them just then and said, "There you are! I was wondering when you'd get here, Phyllis."

Looking at Melissa this morning was a bit more like gazing into that mirror Sam had mentioned. She wore a wig, as Phyllis had suspected she might, and was dressed in a similar outfit of jeans and long-sleeved shirt, although she wore a sweater over the shirt rather than a lightweight jacket. In the novel, Eve hadn't gone into much detail about the sort of clothing each of them usually wore, but evidently the movie's wardrobe department had found enough description to work with. Melissa was still a few inches shorter than Phyllis, of course, and Phyllis still believed she looked younger and more glamorous, but she had to admit that overall the casting was pretty accurate.

"And you brought another pie, too," Melissa went on. "That'll make some people happy, especially Lawrence. He said something earlier this morning about how good that one last night was."

Phyllis didn't say anything about her suspicion that Melissa had sneaked the last piece of pie in the kitchen the night before. If she wanted to pretend that she had resisted temptation, that was fine.

"There's no need for you to carry that around," Sammons said. He lifted a hand, waved to somebody, and called, "Teddy!"

Phyllis expected a young man to respond to that summons, but instead it was a young woman with long dark hair who hurried over. "Yes, Mr. Sammons?" she asked in a voice that sounded very much to Phyllis like it came from Brooklyn.

Sammons took the pie container out of Phyllis's hands and passed it to the young woman. "Take this to the craft services table, but put a hands-off note on it. Lawrence won't happy if somebody else comes along and gobbles it all up before he gets some."

"Sure thing, Mr. Sammons," Teddy said. "Hands off, by order of you."

She hurried off with the pie. Carolyn asked, "Is she an actress?"

"Teddy? No, no, she's a production assistant. An assistant production assistant."

"She's striking."

"Is she?" Sammon said. "I really hadn't noticed."

Phyllis was willing to bet that he had noticed, though. Alan Sammons probably noticed every attractive young female in his vicinity. But if Earl Thorpe could be believed, he behaved himself with them, so Phyllis supposed she couldn't think too badly of him for looking.

He ushered them on toward the crowd

gathered along the lake shore and around the buildings. The vendors' booths where arts, crafts, and food would be sold during the festival were already set up and their signs were in place, because during today's filming everything was supposed to look like it would the next day when the public flocked in here. Orange, brown, and green decorations representing autumn were hung on the buildings and in the trees. Green portable toilets had been brought in and placed around the park, because the regular public restrooms in a rustic stone and wood building wouldn't be enough to handle the crowd at the festival.

As Phyllis, Carolyn, Eve, and Sammons approached one of the old log cabins, Phyllis suddenly tensed as she saw the hay bales stacked in the dogtrot and arranged to form a big seat.

"Oh, dear," Carolyn muttered under her breath, and Phyllis knew she had noticed the bales, too. Both of them slowed and then stopped.

"Something wrong, ladies?" Sammons asked with a frown.

Carolyn said, "It's just that seeing those hay bales . . . I can't help but be reminded . . ."

"They bring back some bad memories,"

Phyllis said. "Of course, we knew that case is the one that Eve used in her book, but to actually see them the way they were that day . . ."

Eve said, "Oh, dear! I've stirred up a lot of painful feelings, and I didn't really mean to do that —"

"No, it's all right, really," Phyllis told her. She summoned up a smile. "After all, I've read your book and it didn't bother me that much."

"Me, either," Carolyn said. "But seeing the scene like this, looking so much like it did, that's more difficult somehow."

Sammons said, "If you'd like to leave, it's perfectly understandable."

Phyllis looked at Eve. She knew Eve wanted her friends to be here today, to share in her success. Phyllis had no intention of letting down a friend, so with a more genuine smile she continued, "No, that's not necessary. I'm fine. Really. And all of this . . ." She waved a hand to take in the hubbub around them. "This experience is so interesting and exciting I wouldn't miss it for the world."

"Yes, I feel the same way," Carolyn added, although she didn't sound quite as sincere as Phyllis did.

A relieved smile appeared on Eve's face.

"I'm glad. But maybe when they bring out the scarecrow prop, it would be a good idea if we didn't watch. When will that be, Alan?"

"I think those shots are on the list for this afternoon," Sammons replied. "I can talk to Lawrence and see if we can rearrange things, if that will help. He probably won't like it, but —"

"You don't have to do that," Phyllis said. "We'll have had more time to get used to it by then, won't we, Carolyn?"

"Of course. This isn't your fault, Eve, so please don't blame yourself."

"It's nobody's fault," Phyllis said. "Just circumstances. And we can deal with circumstances."

Sammons held out a hand and said, "Let's go on and find a good place for you ladies to sit and watch what we're doing this morning, then."

Instead of going on past the log cabin where the hay bales were stacked in the dogtrot, they turned onto another walk and followed it past the iron skeleton of an old covered wagon and some playground equipment toward the cottage where the park's caretaker lived. When they came to a concrete picnic table with benches beside it, Sammons suggested, "How about right here? I'll have some director's chairs brought over for you to sit in, though. They ought to be more comfortable than these benches."

"That's not necessary," Phyllis said. "We'll be fine here, won't we?"

"Yes, I think so," Carolyn said. "Thank you for your consideration, Mr. Sammons."

"Don't mention it," the producer boomed. "We wouldn't even be here if it weren't for you ladies. You were all part of Eve's novel."

Eve nodded and said, "I certainly couldn't have written it without these two. And Sam, of course. Why, nothing really exciting happened until Sam moved in with us."

That was true, Phyllis realized. The first murder in which she had gotten mixed up had been committed shortly before Sam rented the extra room in the house, but they hadn't discovered that it *was* a murder until after he was one of them. And since then . . .

Maybe it was *his* fault all these bizarre things kept happening, Phyllis told herself with a smile. She didn't really believe that . . . but it was an interesting enough idea that she was probably going to tease him about it when she got the chance.

One of the movie crew came up and summoned Alan Sammons to deal with some question or problem mere moments after

Phyllis, Carolyn, and Eve sat down at the picnic table, so they were left to themselves to watch the whirlwind of activity in the park. People scurried everywhere, men shouted to each other and shoved equipment around, and none of it made the least bit of sense to Phyllis.

After a while she saw a large group of people moving around from the other side of the lake, following the road that circled the park. She wondered if those were the extras and searched for Sam and Ronnie among them. Sam hadn't said anything about working as one of the extras, but Phyllis didn't believe for a second that a movie fan like him would pass up an opportunity to appear on screen.

Sam's height and Ronnie's blue hair helped Phyllis pick them out of the crowd. After a minute, Sam spotted her and waved, and that prompted Ronnie to wave, too.

"They look like they're having fun," Eve said. "I may have to get in on that myself before the day is over."

Carolyn said, "Better you than me."

"What do you have against being in a movie?"

"I don't know. The whole thing just seems a little . . . undignified to me. But I never had that urge to be a performer."

"I don't know about that," Phyllis said. "All of us were teachers, after all. We got up in front of an audience every day."

"A captive audience," Carolyn pointed out. "It's not the same thing."

Eve said, "I think Phyllis is right. We had dozens of critics watching us all the time. And a lot of the time they were a hostile audience." She laughed. "I hadn't ever thought of it that way, but there certainly are a lot of similarities."

Carolyn just shook her head, still unwilling to go along with the idea.

Before they could talk about the subject any more, Earl Thorpe hurried past, then stopped abruptly when he realized who they were. "Good morning, ladies," he greeted them. "What do you think of it so far?"

"It's a little on the frantic side, isn't it?"

"This?" Thorpe waved a hand at the crowd. "This is nothing. Everything's going smooth as silk."

"I'm glad to hear it," Eve said.

"Did you get all that work done last night?" Phyllis asked.

"Yeah. You'd be hearing some yelling if I hadn't." Thorpe was wearing some sort of headset with an earpiece in one ear. He lifted a hand to it and pushed the earpiece in better with a finger to help him hear as someone spoke to him. "Be right there," he said into the microphone attached to the headset, then told Phyllis, Carolyn, and Eve, "If you need anything, I'll be around, although you might have trouble catching me."

Eve waved a hand and said, "You just go on about your business, Earl. We wouldn't think of bothering you."

Thorpe smiled, nodded, and hurried off.

"There's Julie," Carolyn said.

They looked where she was pointing and saw not only Julie Cordell but also Heidi Lancaster and Robert Harkness. The three of them were standing about fifty yards away, drinking coffee from styrofoam cups. The casual clothes they wore were actually their wardrobe for the movie, Phyllis guessed. As she watched, Melissa came up and joined them, and looking at the four of them, for a second it *did* seem like she was looking at herself, Sam, Carolyn, and Eve. Alan Sammons had referred to what they were doing here as magic. In some ways, it really was . . .

But if a magic spell had fallen over Holland Lake Park this morning, it was shattered seconds later by a loud, angry voice.

CHAPTER 9

Phyllis turned her head and saw Lawrence Fremont stalking across the park, trailed by the young production assistant Teddy. As he walked, Fremont looked back over his shoulder and continued berating the dark-haired young woman. He had some rolled-up papers in his right hand, and he punctuated his angry words by slapping them sharply against his left palm.

Fremont's tirade had caused many of the surrounding conversations to quiet down, so Phyllis was able to make out some of what he was saying.

". . . amateurish . . . terrible lines . . . find . . . bring them to me . . ."

Phyllis wondered if that was a copy of the script he was holding. From the sound of it, he wasn't happy with something Jason and Deanne Wilkes had written and wanted to talk to them. If that was the case, Phyllis wouldn't have wanted to be in the couple's shoes.

The talk welled back up again as Fremont passed. Teddy turned and scurried off to carry out his orders. Fremont went down to the edge of the lake and stood there flipping through the pages he held. A few minutes later, Teddy approached him again, and as Phyllis suspected, she had Jason and Deanne with her.

Fremont turned and confronted the screenwriters. He waved the pages, which appeared to be paper-clipped together, then started jabbing his finger at them in different places, clearly pointing out things he didn't like. Jason and Deanne both responded rapidly, probably trying to explain something, but Fremont kept talking over them.

Finally, he took the paperclip off the pages and threw them up wildly in the air. They scattered, some landing on the bank but others flying out over the lake and landing on the water, where they floated. That display of anger made people fall silent again. Fremont stomped off, leaving Jason and Deanne to stand beside the lake looking dejected.

Then Deanne turned to her husband and spoke to him in obvious anger. Jason countered with a shrug, which just made Deanne madder. She walked off, too. Jason stood there by himself now as he took off his glasses, rubbed wearily at his temples, and let out a visible sigh. No one approached him, perhaps not wanting any of Fremont's anger to rub off on them.

After a moment, Jason put the glasses back on and started picking up the pages lying on the ground around him. He didn't try to retrieve the ones floating in the lake. Somebody would have to get a pole of some sort and fish them out, Phyllis thought. They wouldn't want paper floating around out there to get in any of the shots.

"My goodness," Eve said.

"Is that the first time you've seen him blow his stack like that?" Carolyn asked.

"Yes. I've heard stories about his temper, of course, but . . . Oh, my, I feel sorry for Jason and Deanne. I wonder what they wrote to set him off like that."

Phyllis said, "From the way Deanne was acting after Fremont stomped off, more likely it was Jason who wrote what he didn't like."

"You mean she threw him under the bus," Carolyn said.

"Well . . . that's what it looked like."

"I got the same impression."

As Phyllis watched, Teddy came up to Jason Wilkes and spoke to him, then put a hand on his arm. Jason nodded and forced a smile onto his face. They walked off together. Teddy's solicitous attitude and Jason's response to it made Phyllis wonder if the young production assistant had anything to do with the friction between Jason and Deanne. Eve had chalked up that argument to creative differences, but that might not be all that was going on.

Things quickly got back to normal after that incident. Phyllis supposed that with so much to do, the movie-makers had no choice but to put such disturbances behind them and move on.

She saw Earl Thorpe hurrying around, talking to members of the crew working with the cameras and lights, pointing and arranging things and giving orders as if he were directing this movie, not Lawrence Fremont. She hadn't seen Fremont again after the fit he'd pitched with Jason and Deanne Wilkes.

The extras began to spread out through the park, and members of the crew drew back to the edges. Phyllis took that to mean that shooting was about to get underway. She had seen Thorpe talking to the extras, evidently giving them instructions. She noticed that as they began to mill around, no one looked toward the cameras, so Thorpe must have warned them about that. People moved along the walkways and stood in front of the vendors' booths, children scrambled around and climbed on the playground equipment, young couples held hands. Phyllis had been to enough of the real Harvest Festivals to tell that this was a reasonable approximation of what went on at one of them. She wondered if the cameras were already rolling, getting background shots that could be edited into the movie later.

More activity, this time in the parking lot, caught her attention. When she turned to get a better look, she saw that Lawrence Fremont had reappeared and was standing beside a large camera with several other people. Vehicles had been moved, leaving several open parking spaces that hadn't been there earlier. As Phyllis watched, a Lincoln sedan similar to hers pulled into one of the spaces and stopped. The doors opened and Melissa Keller and Julie Cordell got out. They closed the car doors and walked toward the camera.

Phyllis hadn't heard Fremont say "Action", nor did she hear him say "Cut", but from the way Melissa and Julie stopped and turned back to the car, she knew the director had ended the scene. Fremont walked over to them and spoke for a moment, then they got back into the car. Melissa backed out of the space as Fremont returned to the camera.

Then it all happened again, Melissa parking and the two of them getting out and walking into the park.

And again.

Phyllis frowned. She couldn't understand why Fremont was making them do the simple little scene over and over again. As far as she'd been able to tell, it was just fine the first time. Clearly Fremont had seen something about it that he didn't like, though.

By the fifth time they did the shot, Phyllis could tell from the body language Melissa and Julie were exhibiting that they were getting tired of it. She could see their frustration. Maybe Fremont was able to recognize that, too, because he waved them on, and after the camera was turned and set up again, he shot several more scenes of them walking in various places in the park. He made them repeat some of those as well, for no apparent reason that Phyllis could see.

Meanwhile, off to the side, Robert Harkness and Heidi Lancaster were standing around with their hands in their pockets, since the air was a little cool this morning. They talked to each other and looked bored. Phyllis decided that she wouldn't want to be an actor. Talk about hurry up and wait . . .

After a while, Harkness got into a scene. He ran up to Melissa and threw his arms around her as "Tom" comforted "Peggy". It was quite an emphatic embrace, more demonstrative than Sam would be in a situation like that. But things were always a little larger than life in movies, Phyllis supposed. As she watched, she could believe that Harkness's character really cared for Melissa's and had been worried about her. That was good acting, since the two of them didn't like each other in real life.

Actors wearing police uniforms appeared, hurrying here and there as the camera followed them. Lawrence Fremont supervised some of those scenes, barking orders and making the actors do things over again. For other shots, Earl Thorpe appeared to be in charge, and those went more quickly and efficiently. Phyllis wondered if Fremont knew the assistant director was actually helming some of those scenes, to use the terminology she had heard Sam use. She was curious, as well, if Alan Sammons had told Thorpe to do that to speed things up, since Lawrence Fremont didn't seem to be in any hurry to get much done today.

After a while, a slender, very attractive young woman with long dark hair pulled into a ponytail that hung down her back appeared. She wore a trench coat, and as soon as Phyllis saw her, she felt like she knew the woman. After a few minutes, she realized why. Although her hair was longer, the young woman resembled Isabel Largo, the Weatherford Police Department detective who had investigated the murder that actually took place here.

Fremont went over to her and spoke intensely to her. As he did, he put his hand on her arm and moved it up and down in a caressing fashion. The young woman didn't pull away. Remembering what Thorpe had told her the night before, Phyllis took out her phone and searched the name Becca Peterson. The images that came up confirmed her guess. Becca Peterson was the actress playing the role based on Detective Largo . . . the actress who was thinking about going public with her accusations of harassment against Lawrence Fremont.

Just by looking at the two of them now, it didn't appear that a problem existed between them, but Phyllis knew how deceptive appearances could be. Fremont seemed to be trying to be friendly, but Becca Peterson remained cool and professional. She nodded and performed the scene again the way Fremont wanted her to.

While that was going on, Earl Thorpe shot scenes that involved extras and bit part players running around and looking frightened. Eve pointed that out and said, "Those must be reaction shots for after the body's been discovered."

Carolyn grimaced. "It was a madhouse, all right."

"Look," Phyllis said, "there's Sam and Ronnie again."

Thorpe waved them over and spoke to them. Ronnie clapped her hands to her cheeks and opened her mouth in a wide "O" as if she were screaming. Thorpe handed her a piece of paper and pointed to something printed on it.

"They're giving her a line," Eve said as she leaned forward eagerly.

"She's never expressed any interest in acting before now, as far as I know," Phyllis said. "She seems pretty excited about it, though."

"I just hope she doesn't get carried away with all sorts of crazy ideas and dreams," Carolyn said.

"Ronnie is pretty level-headed."

"She has *blue* hair. And don't forget everything that happened when she ran away from home and came all the way down here all because of some boy."

"Well, she's still a teenager," Phyllis admitted. "She can be impulsive. But Sam's her grandfather."

"Yes, and maybe if he lives long enough, *he'll* grow up one of these days, too."

That comment irritated Phyllis a little, but she didn't say anything. At times, Sam did display a certain amount of boyish enthusiasm that was at odds with his actual age. Maybe too much boyish enthusiasm. But that was just part of who he was and Phyllis liked that about him. He made her feel younger.

Lawrence Fremont strode up to Thorpe, Ronnie, and Sam while the assistant director was still talking to Ronnie. Rather curtly, he took the page of script out of Ronnie's hand, pulled a pen from his shirt pocket, and emphatically crossed something out, then scribbled a replacement line and gave the page back to her. Ronnie frowned as she read it, then she looked up and spoke. Phyllis assumed she was reading the line.

Fremont shook his head and motioned for her to do it again. Ronnie did so, and this time Fremont moved closer to her and slipped his arm around her shoulders. He leaned his head over until it was almost touching hers as he spoke. He motioned animatedly with his other hand.

"Now wait just a minute . . ." Carolyn muttered.

Phyllis had the same reaction. She didn't care for the intimate way Fremont had forced himself into Ronnie's personal space. She put her hands on the picnic table and got ready to stand up. She didn't want to march across the park and make a scene, but Fremont needed to back off.

Of course, she didn't have to do a thing, she realized a moment later, because Sam was right there and moved in close on Ronnie's other side. He had a friendly look on his face, and when he reached over and put a hand on Fremont's arm, it was a comradely gesture, but Phyllis knew the casual grip was about to turn steely and remove the director's arm from Ronnie's shoulders.

Fremont didn't let it get that far. Smoothly, he disengaged and moved back a step, then pointed to the script page in Ronnie's hand again and put a smile on his face. The damage control worked. She smiled back at him and nodded. Fremont said something to Earl Thorpe and then walked away.

"Thank goodness," Eve said in a relieved tone, indicating that she had been watching the incident, too. "I was afraid Sam was going to punch him."

"Sam wouldn't have done that," Phyllis said. "Fremont is half his size. But he *would* have made sure the man left Ronnie alone." She looked at Eve. "That could have ruined everything."

"You mean about the movie?" Eve shook her head. "Oh, no, don't worry about that. I'm thrilled that they're making it, but Sam and Ronnie are more important than any movie. All of you are my friends. My family, if you get right down to it."

"And we feel the same way," Carolyn said. "Still, I'm glad it seems to have blown over."

Phyllis was, too. Thorpe ushered Sam and Ronnie over to join some of the other extras and started setting up the camera for the shot that would include them . . . and Ronnie's movie debut. She wondered idly if having a speaking part, even one line, meant that Ronnie would be paid more.

She was musing about that when she looked across the park and saw Lawrence Fremont again. The director had stopped and was looking intently back at the area where Ronnie and Sam were. The gaze

109

lasted only a moment before he turned away, but while it did, Fremont's expression was furious.

CHAPTER 10

With the steady stream of activity going on around them, time actually passed pretty quickly. Almost before Phyllis realized it, it was the middle of the day and time for the movie company to break for lunch. Alan Sammons came up to the picnic table where they were sitting and said, "You ladies come with me. You can eat at the craft services table."

"Won't that get you in trouble?" Eve asked. "That food is supposed to be for the cast and crew. We're not members of any union."

"There's not a retired teachers' union?" Sammons asked with a grin.

"Teachers have professional organizations," Carolyn said. "It's not exactly the same thing."

"Yeah, well, you come on with me." Sammons laughed. "Who's gonna tell me no? I'm the producer!"

As they started across the park with him, Phyllis said, "I don't mean any offense, Mr. Sammons —"

"Alan. And people who start off by saying they don't mean any offense usually do."

"Alan," Phyllis said. "And I really don't."

"I know that. I'm just giving you the business."

"What I was going to say," Phyllis went on, "is that you don't seem like what I'd think of as a movie producer. I mean, you're . . ."

"A nice guy?" Sammons laughed again. "Believe me, I know exactly what you mean. Some guys, when they're in such a high-pressure business, they get used to the pace and the hard-nosed attitudes they have to take, and they never really turn it off. But some of us, we come from normal back-grounds — I grew up in a small town in Kansas, for example — and we remember what it's like to deal with regular people. This whole experience, it's like a breath of fresh air for me. I'm glad to get out of L.A. now and then. And I'm not just talking about the pollution when I say that about fresh air."

"We really appreciate the way you're taking care of us and trying to make a good movie," Eve said. "It can't be easy, with so many different personalities to take into account. Strong personalities, at that."

"It's no harder than juggling chainsaws."

They came to the craft services table, which was actually several portable tables set up and covered with food. Sandwiches, fried chicken, fruit, chips, donuts, cookies . . . nothing fancy, just food to get hardworking people through the day. Phyllis saw her pie container at the end of one table. It had a large sticky note on it warning people to keep their hands off, by order of the producer.

A large crowd was already on hand, lining up to fill paper plates with food and get plastic cups full of tea or foam cups of coffee. Sammons, Phyllis, Carolyn, and Eve got in line along with everyone else.

"When it comes to craft services," Sammons explained, "we're very egalitarian. A producer's no more important than a grip or a boom mic operator. Everybody has a job to do, so everybody eats."

"What about the extras?" Phyllis asked. She had looked around for Sam and Ronnie but didn't see them nearby.

"We have box lunches for them. Admittedly, it's not much. A plain sandwich, a bag of chips, and an apple. A tub of canned drinks. But it's better than nothing." Understanding suddenly dawned on the man's broad face. "You're thinking about Sam and his granddaughter. They'd be welcome here, too, but they probably don't know to come over. I'll send somebody to find them."

He started looking around for some assistant to assign the task to, but before he could find anybody, Phyllis said, "Never mind. I see them. They're headed this way."

Sam and Ronnie weaved through the crowd toward them, each carrying a small white cardboard box. As they came up, Sammons told them, "You guys don't have to eat that lunch if you don't want to —"

"Shoot, no, it's fine," Sam said. "We're extras, so we'll chow down like extras, right, Ronnie?"

"Sure, I guess," the girl said. She smiled and added, "I do have a line, though, so I'm a bit player."

Phyllis wanted to talk to her about that, but not in the middle of this mob. She looked around, spied an empty picnic table, and pointed to it.

"Why don't the two of you go sit over there," she suggested, "and we'll join you in a minute."

"Sounds good to me," Sam agreed.

Phyllis and the others got their food, but before they could join Sam and Ronnie,

114

Teddy the assistant production assistant hurried up and said, "Mr. Sammons, Mr. Fremont wants to talk to you."

Sammons rolled his eyes, but he nodded and said, "Okay, Teddy, tell him I'll be right there." He smiled and went on, "I'll see you later, ladies. Enjoy the rest of the shooting."

They carried their plates and cups over to the picnic table and sat down with Sam and Ronnie, who had the boxed lunches open. The sandwiches didn't look that appetizing, Phyllis noted. She said, "If I had thought about it, I'd have fixed lunches for us and brought them along."

"We won't starve," Sam said. "How are you likin' it so far? Havin' fun?"

"There's an awful lot going on," Carolyn said. "It's rather difficult to keep up with."

"We saw that conversation between you and Mr. Fremont, though," Phyllis said to Ronnie.

The girl's eyes dropped to the boxed lunch on the table in front of her. "Yeah, that was kind of crazy, wasn't it?" she said with a forced note of humor in her voice. "All over one silly line in a movie script."

"What *was* the line?" Eve asked.

"Well, the way it was written, I was supposed to scream a little and then yell, 'Somebody's been murdered!' But Mr.

Fremont changed it and wanted me to say, 'Somebody's dead!' He said it was entirely different."

"Actually, it is," Phyllis said. "I take it this is going to be on screen right after the body is discovered?"

"Yeah, when everybody's running around and panicking."

Phyllis glanced at Carolyn, knew that she was remembering that day, too, and said, "At that point, we didn't know the victim had been murdered. All anybody knew was that he was dead. It took a while before enough evidence was gathered to conclude that the death was a homicide. So technically Mr. Fremont was right."

"That makes sense, I guess," Ronnie said with a shrug. "It didn't matter to me which word I yelled. All Mr. Fremont had to do was cross it out and change it. But he seemed to think that it was some sort of big deal, and that the Wilkeses had really messed up by writing it that way. They didn't even know for sure they were going to need to write a line for me until last night."

"And there was certainly no reason for the man to paw you that way," Carolyn said. "I thought Phyllis was going to charge across there and slap him silly."

116

Ronnie blushed, but she looked at Phyllis and said, "I'm glad you didn't. I can take care of myself. It was bad enough that Granddad kind of pushed Mr. Fremont away."

"I didn't push him," Sam said. "If I'd pushed him, he'd've known it."

"Anyway, he was just making sure I understood how he wanted me to deliver the line."

"How many ways can you shout 'Someone's dead'?" Carolyn wanted to know.

"He said I needed to have just the right amount of fright and panic in my voice," Ronnie explained. "That makes sense, doesn't it?"

"I suppose it does," Phyllis said, "and it's over now, so the best thing to do is for all of us to forget about it and enjoy the rest of the day. You already shot that part, right?"

"Yep," Sam said. "It's in the can. You did a great job, too, didn't you, Ronnie?"

The girl grinned. "Academy Award nomination, sure thing. Best scream by a completely amateur actress." She paused. "I'm kind of enjoying it, though. It's too late for me to take any drama classes in high school, but there are little theater groups around, aren't there? Maybe I could do something like that next summer and then look into

117

taking some real classes when I start college."

"If that's what you want," Sam said.

Ronnie looked at Phyllis again. "Did you really want to slug Mr. Fremont when he started getting a little handsy?"

"I'm a lady," Phyllis said. "I've never slugged anybody."

That avoided answering the question of whether or not she had *wanted* to. Ronnie didn't seem to notice that, though.

Once lunch was finished, everyone went back to work without any delay. Time was money, as Alan Sammons had said, and as Sam put it, "We're burnin' daylight. They got to have it to shoot these scenes." He and Ronnie went down to the lake where the extras were assembling again.

Since Phyllis, Carolyn, and Eve could still see everything from this table, they stayed where they were. Phyllis watched as Earl Thorpe set up some shots and got them on film. She didn't see Lawrence Fremont but supposed he was around somewhere.

"Mind if I join you, ladies?"

Phyllis looked around and saw Deanne Wilkes standing beside the table. Eve said, "No, of course not," and waved to the empty space beside her on the bench. "Are you all right, Deanne?"

The woman managed a smile as she sat down and said, "You mean, after that humiliating debacle earlier this morning that was all Jason's fault? Sure, I'm fine. I'm used to it by now, or at least I should be."

"Mr. Fremont does have a temper, all right," Eve said.

Deanne shook her head. "I was talking about Jason screwing something up and getting us in trouble. That's happening all the time lately. He's . . . distracted."

Phyllis wondered if that distraction was in the form of a certain dark-haired production assistant with a Brooklyn accent.

Deanne went on, "I'm working on getting some projects of my own lined up. You don't have any other novels in the works, do you, Eve?"

"I've been thinking about a sequel," Eve admitted. "I don't particularly want to be known as a one-book author."

Deanne shook her head. "No, you need to write something a lot darker and grittier. A psychological thriller. Have you read any books by those Scandinavian authors? They have complex plots, but there's lot of brooding and depression, too."

Carolyn said, "If I lived somewhere it was

always gloomy and snowing, I'd be depressed, too."

As if she hadn't heard the comment, Deanne went on, "You caught lightning in a bottle with your first book, Eve, but there's no guarantee you could do it again. That's why you have to study the market and write what people want."

Phyllis thought that if she ever sat down to write a book, she wouldn't put in so much hard work unless she was writing what *she* wanted to, and then she would worry about trying to sell it, just as Eve had done the first time around. But that was just her, she told herself. It was entirely up to Eve what she did next.

"I'll think about it," Eve promised.

Deanne nodded. "And see if you can come up with something that has the word 'girl' in the title. In fact, maybe we should brainstorm and come up with a good marketable title, and then you can figure out the book that goes with it."

"That's a good idea," Eve said, but Phyllis could tell that her friend wasn't all that enthusiastic about it.

"I'll think about it and email you," Deanne said.

Earl Thorpe walked by, looking quickly from side to side as if he were searching for someone. He confirmed that by stopping and asking, "Have any of you ladies seen Lawrence?"

Phyllis thought about it and said, "Not since before lunch, actually."

"I've been avoiding him," Deanne said.

Thorpe grunted. "I don't blame you." He looked at Carolyn and Eve, and they shook their heads.

"We've been right here with Phyllis," Carolyn said. "Mr. Fremont hasn't come around."

Thorpe frowned and said, "Nobody saw him come to the craft services table for lunch, either. He might have gone back to his motor home and fallen asleep, but that wouldn't be like him." He sighed. "Guess I'll have to go and check, though. We're ready to shoot the scene with the scarecrow, down there at the cabin, and that's important enough he's not gonna want anybody else doing that."

Thorpe hurried toward the road and the motor homes parked on the other side. Deanne watched him go and said, "I feel sorry for Earl. He's a talented guy and deserves more credit than he gets for working with Lawrence. If you ask me, he should be the one to direct *The Bancroft Inheritance.*"

"What's that?" Phyllis asked.

"Lawrence's next movie. *Not* from a script that Jason and I wrote, by the way." Deanne stood up. "I suppose I should go find Jason. I've been avoiding him, too. He's probably huddled in a corner somewhere sulking, the poor baby, instead of trying to fix the things in the script that had Lawrence so upset." As she walked off, she looked over her shoulder and added, "I'll email you about those ideas, Eve."

Once Deanne was out of earshot, Carolyn shook her head and said, "I don't believe that marriage is going to last."

"I hate to say it, but I agree with you," Eve said. "They weren't really that well-matched to start with, I suppose, and the pressures of living and working in Hollywood are an awful lot for any couple to cope with, even the good ones."

The afternoon's activities had started off at a rather frantic pace, which seemed to be par for the course when it came to movie-making, but now they slowed and an air of anticipation settled over the park. Phyllis wondered if that was because the scarecrow scene was an important one, and it couldn't proceed until Lawrence Fremont showed up. She looked around for Becca Peterson but didn't see the striking actress anywhere.

Maybe Fremont was in his motor home with her. If that was the case, he wouldn't appreciate having Earl Thorpe knock on his door. They might be on the verge of another blow-up.

Melissa and Julie walked over to the picnic table. Both of them looked impatient. Melissa said, "I really shouldn't be surprised, but I can't believe Lawrence is making us all stand around and wait like this."

"He probably thinks it's funny," Julie said. "You know how he is. And then if anybody says anything to him about it, he'll fly off the handle."

"Good grief!" Carolyn said. "If he's always so much trouble, why does anyone hire him to direct a movie?"

"Because they make money," Melissa said, "and because they usually get good reviews and get talked about when awards season comes around. It's a bottom-line business, but it's fueled by egos, too, and Lawrence's pictures hit both of those marks . . . no matter how much of an ass he is."

Julie said, "Alan's about to have a stroke. If Lawrence doesn't turn up soon, he's going to order Earl to go ahead and direct the scene. Then things will *really* hit the fan when Lawrence finds out about it."

Eve shook her head and said, "I'm glad

my part in this is long since over with."

Melissa smiled. "Hey, what would a movie location be without some drama, right?"

Phyllis looked past the two actresses and saw Earl Thorpe and Alan Sammons coming toward them. She said, "I think something is about to happen."

Melissa looked over her shoulder and said, "Uh-oh. You're right."

The two men came up to the table. Sammons announced heavily, "Lawrence isn't in his motor home, and we can't find him. So we're going to go ahead and shoot the scarecrow scene since everything is ready. Earl will handle it."

"You know he's not going to like that," Melissa said.

Sammons nodded. "I know. But I'll take full responsibility. Are the two of you ready?"

"Sure," Julie said. "We're just waiting for somebody to say 'action'."

"I'll do that," Thorpe said grimly.

"Wish us luck," Melissa said to Phyllis, Carolyn, and Eve. "You want to come along and get a closer look?"

"Not at all," Carolyn replied without hesitation. "We saw the real thing, remember?"

"And in close-up," Phyllis added. "But

good luck."

The group walked off, and Eve said, "Should we have told them to break a leg? Or is that only in the theater?"

"I don't know," Phyllis said. She thought she could look it up on her phone, then decided not to. It was all right not to know everything, after all.

From where they were sitting, they could see into the dogtrot where the hay bales were arranged, but the angle was such that they couldn't see the prop scarecrow itself, only the top of its head in a battered old hat sticking up over one of the bales. Phyllis's eyes were drawn to that despite the bad memories that kept trying to float to the surface of her thoughts.

She wasn't the only one. "I can't stop looking down there," Carolyn murmured.

"Neither can I," Eve said. "Honestly, that scene in the book creeped me out a little when I wrote it. I'm glad I didn't have to . . . well, live it."

"This shouldn't take long," Phyllis said. "We know that Mr. Thorpe won't make them do it over and over again like Mr. Fremont might have. And then they'll move on to something else."

"Fine with me," Carolyn said.

Phyllis watched as Thorpe, Melissa, and

Julie stood at one side of the dogtrot. Thorpe gestured as he talked to the two women. He was explaining to them how he wanted them to walk into the scene and what to do next, Phyllis could tell that much. Melissa and Julie nodded. Thorpe went to the far side of the dogtrot where the camera and lights were set up. Melissa and Julie moved back so they would be out of the shot when the camera began rolling.

The second assistant director slated the shot. Everyone had fallen silent now, so the sharp noise of the clapper coming down on the slate could be heard throughout the park. Phyllis heard Thorpe call, "Action."

Melissa and Julie walked toward the bales. Phyllis could hear them saying their lines to each other, although she couldn't make out all the words. Honestly, she didn't remember what she and Carolyn had said on that day. They had been talking about the festival, she recalled, but Eve had made up their dialogue when writing the book and then that dialogue had been adapted further in the script by Jason and Deanne Wilkes, so it wasn't exactly like it had been in real life.

There were other differences as well, Phyllis realized. She frowned and said, "The scarecrow was standing up when it happened, with a pole through his clothes to keep him upright. That's the way you wrote it in the book, Eve."

"Yes, but it's easier to film with him sitting down," Eve said. "That's what Jason and Deanne told me. They change a lot of things in a movie because it's easier."

"I suppose," Phyllis said. She knew logically that it didn't matter. The scene would still be very dramatic.

Down in the dogtrot, Melissa and Julie turned to the scarecrow, and Melissa reached out to adjust the way the prop was sitting. Phyllis leaned forward, knowing this was when "Peggy Nelson" would discover the scarecrow was really a corpse.

Suddenly, Melissa leaped backward. A scream ripped from her mouth.

"Goodness!" Carolyn exclaimed. "She's really putting a lot into it."

Phyllis caught her breath as Melissa continued to scream. She backpedaled away from the scarecrow so fast she stumbled, lost her balance, and sat down hard on the ground.

And all the time she was still screaming . . .

Phyllis, Carolyn, and Eve were on their feet without even thinking about it. Down in the cabin, Earl Thorpe rushed into the dogtrot, caught hold of Melissa, and pulled her up. She buried her face against his chest, but Phyllis could still hear her screams as other members of the cast and crew swarmed around the dogtrot.

"Something's actually wrong down there," Carolyn said.

Phyllis agreed . . . and she had a sinking feeling that she knew what it was.

CHAPTER 11

Phyllis's next thought was to look around for Sam and Ronnie. She didn't know where they had been when Melissa started screaming. She had no reason to think that they weren't all right, but she wanted to see them with her own eyes and be sure.

Within seconds, she spotted Sam and his granddaughter hurrying toward them. Sam had hold of Ronnie's hand so he wouldn't get separated from her as the crowd in the park began panicking.

Not everyone reacted that way, of course. During the morning's shooting, pretend panic had been common, and clearly some of the extras believed this was just more of the same. They just looked curiously toward the log cabins, trying to see what was going on.

But there was something so real about Melissa's screams, so filled with dread, that the feeling proved contagious and a good number of the people crowded into the park started trying to get out of there as quickly as possible.

"What in blazes happened?" Sam asked as he and Ronnie joined Phyllis, Carolyn, and Eve beside the picnic table.

"We couldn't see what was going on from where we were," Ronnie added.

"I don't know," Phyllis said. "Melissa and Julie were doing their scene with the scarecrow when Melissa jumped back, fell down, and started screaming."

Carolyn said, "I know what it means. There's been a murder. I'm sure of it."

Eve stared at her. "In the same place? Involving a scarecrow again? That's insane!"

"Think about it," Carolyn said grimly. "What else can it be?"

Phyllis was very much afraid that her old friend was probably right. It didn't pay to ignore the lessons of history . . . and as a retired history teacher, Phyllis knew that better than most!

"Well, I'm gonna go down there and find out," Sam said. "Ronnie, you stay here."

"Sam, wait a minute," Phyllis said. She had seen Alan Sammons hurry up to the dogtrot and wave his arms around wildly, and now several burly men in windbreakers appeared as if out of nowhere and took up positions around the cabin. Phyllis saw the word SECURITY on the back of the wind-breakers. She didn't know where these men had been all day — she hadn't noticed them around the park — but they must have been here, keeping a low profile. You couldn't shoot a movie with a lot of stars and expensive equipment and not have security around, she realized. The company's insurance policy would have required that.

She went on, "They're not going to let anyone get too close to . . . whatever it is . . . and that's a good thing. I'm sure someone has called the police by now."

The wail of a siren not too far away followed her words by a matter of seconds, confirming what she'd said. Now things would fall into an all too familiar pattern: uniformed officers would arrive at the park, followed soon by detectives and crime scene techs and probably the chief of police himself, since this was destined to be a high-profile case.

She was just assuming that Carolyn was right and that someone had been murdered, she told herself. But the same thought had occurred to her before Carolyn ever gave voice to it.

By now the idea that something bad actually had happened had spread throughout the park. The ominous presence of the security personnel around the log cabin must have convinced everyone who didn't believe it at first. And as the frantic mass exodus continued, Carolyn muttered, "I'll bet the killer is getting away right now in all this confusion."

"Could be, but there's too many people here to keep 'em corralled," Sam said.

"We shouldn't leave, should we?" Ronnie asked.

Phyllis said, "No, we'll stay right here so we can cooperate with the investigation. Not that there'll much we can do to help. I don't know where you and Sam were, but the three of us were sitting here a good fifty yards away."

"We were over by that old wagon," Ronnie said.

Sam added, "When the second AD called for everybody to be quiet, we just stayed right there where we were and watched what we could, which wasn't much."

Flashing lights appeared in the parking lot as a couple of police cruisers pulled in. A pair of uniformed officers got out of each car and trotted down through the park toward the log cabin. Alan Sammons met them, talking quickly and pointing back toward the dogtrot. He was clearly upset and kept stopping to scrub a hand over his face. He looked like he wanted to start pulling his hair out.

Melissa wasn't screaming anymore. Phyllis tried to look past the security guards to see if she could spot the actress. She thought she saw Melissa standing with Julie Cordell and Earl Thorpe near the log cabin, but with such a crowd around, she couldn't be sure.

Then a couple of the security men stepped aside to let Sammons and two of the police officers past, and Phyllis got a good look at Melissa. She was pale and obviously shaken, but she seemed to be in control of herself again. Julie stood beside her with an arm around her shoulders in support, as Carolyn would have been if it were the two of them down there.

"Who do you think got murdered?" Ronnie asked in a hushed voice.

"We don't know that anyone did," Eve pointed out.

Carolyn's dismissive snort made it clear what she thought about that statement.

Phyllis said, "We don't really know anything, but I'm sure we'll find out eventually. When the detectives get here, they'll start canvassing the crowd. They'll talk to us sooner or later."

"You know all of them, don't you?" Ronnie said.

Phyllis shook her head. "Hardly. I've had dealings with a few of them, that's all."

She had annoyed the police detectives by getting involved in murder cases, then aggravated those feelings by figuring out who the killers were before the authorities were able to. Those were the 'dealings' she referred to.

"Too bad this isn't in the sheriff's jurisdiction. Mike could fill us in, I'll bet."

Phyllis's son Mike was a Parker County sheriff's deputy and had risked his job on numerous occasions in the past to help her get to the bottom of some murder. She was just as glad that Mike *wouldn't* be involved in this case.

And there was no real reason for her to be, either, she reminded herself, except as a witness . . . and a very minor one at that. Whichever detective wound up questioning her, she could lay out everything she knew in a matter of a few minutes.

More police cruisers showed up. Uniformed officers established a perimeter around the park. Dozens of people who had been here when the trouble broke out had already left, but at least a hundred were still on hand and the police had no intention of letting them go until they had been questioned. The rest of the afternoon would be busy indeed.

"We might as well sit down," Phyllis told the others. "It's probably going to be a while before they get around to us."

They hadn't been waiting long when Phyllis saw a tall, dark-haired woman enter the park. She thought for a second the woman was Becca Peterson, who she had seen with Lawrence Fremont earlier in the day. Then she realized that this woman was dressed in jeans and a black double rider leather jacket and had shorter hair. This was a case of life imitating art instead of the other way around. Detective Isabel Largo strode along one of the winding concrete walks toward the log cabin.

Detective Largo stopped short, though, as she glanced toward the table where Phyllis and the others were sitting. Then she changed course and came in their direction instead.

"Uh-oh," Sam said. "I think the detective looks a mite unhappy."

"Mrs. Newsom," Largo said sharply as she came up to the table. "What are you doing here?"

Phyllis stood up and said, "We were invited. Mr. Sammons, the producer, asked us to come and watch the filming today as his guests."

"That's the only reason?" Largo asked with a frown.

"Why else would we be here?"

"You've got to admit, you *do* seem to turn up at a lot of murder scenes."

Carolyn said, "Then there *was* a murder. I knew it. Who's the victim?"

Largo didn't answer that question. She said, "All of you stay here. I'll be back to talk to you later."

"We won't go anywhere," Phyllis promised.

The detective turned and walked toward the log cabin again. Ronnie watched her go and said, "She acts like she's suspicious of you."

"Most of the police resent Phyllis because she's solved all those murders they couldn't," Carolyn said. "She's kept a lot of innocent people from going to jail." She looked at Eve. "We know that from experience, don't we?"

"We certainly do," Eve said.

"And Phyllis has been behind bars herself," Sam added. "Of course, that didn't work out too well for the district attorney when she made a fool out of him later on."

Phyllis started to say, "I didn't make a fool

out of —" when Ronnie interrupted her.

"You've been in *jail*?" the girl asked, wide-eyed. "Wow. I didn't know you were such a bad —"

"Wait a minute," Sam broke in. "All those folks down there are lookin' at us."

Phyllis turned toward the log cabin and saw that the people gathered near the dogtrot were indeed staring up the little hill toward the picnic table. Standing in the middle of the group were Isabel Largo and Melissa Keller, and the actress had her arm raised with her finger pointing right at Phyllis, who heard her say distinctly, "There she is. That's who you want to talk to — Phyllis Newsom!"

CHAPTER 12

"Wait just a doggone minute," Sam said. "Is she tryin' to say that you had somethin' to do with whatever happened, Phyllis?"

"I don't know," Phyllis replied. "I don't see how that would be possible. We were all the way up here and haven't even been close to the cabin and the dogtrot all day."

Carolyn said, "But with so many people in the park and all the confusion going on constantly, how would we ever prove that?" The others all looked at her in surprise, prompting her to add, "What? I'm just playing the devil's advocate and saying what the police are bound to be thinking."

"We alibi each other," Eve pointed out. "We know where we've been the whole time."

Alibis provided by long-time friends and housemates might not be regarded as reliable evidence, though, and Phyllis knew that. Still, without even being sure exactly what had happened, such speculation was a waste of time.

Detective Largo spoke to one of the uniformed officers, who hurried across the park to the picnic table. "The detective would like for you and your friends to come down to the log cabin, ma'am," he said to Phyllis.

"All right." She followed the officer and the others trailed behind her.

When they reached the area near the log cabin, Phyllis said to Largo, "I thought you were going to question us later, Detective."

"Yes, well, that was the plan, but Ms. Keller here insisted that we talk to you now," Largo answered. "She doesn't want to answer questions until you're on hand."

"That's right," Melissa said. "I'd rather just tell the story once, so I want you to hear it, too, Phyllis. If anybody's going to solve this, it's going to be you."

"Now wait just a minute —" Phyllis began.

"Civilians aren't allowed to interfere with police investigations," Largo said.

Melissa gave her a tolerant look. "Really? I did my research for this part, Detective. I know how it works around here. You may investigate the crime, but it's Phyllis who solves it."

She was just making things worse, Phyllis

thought. She wished Melissa would just answer Detective Largo's questions, whatever they were. Melissa was still shaken up, though, with red-rimmed eyes and a blotchy face from crying, and if Phyllis could make her feel better by being here, she was willing to do that.

With a visible effort at controlling her irritation and impatience, Isabel Largo said, "Why don't we step over here, and you can tell me what happened from the beginning. All right, Ms. Keller?"

"Of course," Melissa said. "I want to help."

Largo inclined her head to Phyllis and said, "You come along, too."

Julie and Thorpe would have followed as Largo led Melissa and Phyllis along the side of the cabin toward its end, but a couple of officers moved in front of them, one saying, "If you folks would just wait here, please."

Phyllis motioned for Sam and the others to stay where they were, too. She knew that Detective Largo didn't want a crowd around while she was questioning Melissa, and she wanted the actress away from her friends, too. Everyone would be questioned separately.

The fact that Phyllis was being included now meant that Largo actually *didn't* regard her as a suspect of any sort. Phyllis was pleased by that, anyway. She had been under clouds of suspicion enough times in her life.

"All right," Largo said to Melissa once the three of them were alone at the end of the cabin, next to an old, non-working well. "Start at the first."

"Of this scene, you mean?"

"When you walked up to the dogtrot where the hay bales and the scarecrow are."

"Well, Julie and I walked up to the cabin and into the dogtrot after Earl said 'action' —"

"Earl?"

"Earl Thorpe, the director. Assistant director, actually, but he was in charge of this scene because . . ."

Melissa's voice trailed off and a shudder ran through her.

"Go on," Largo said.

"Do you know the plot of this movie?"

"I've read Ms. Turner's book," the detective said, which surprised Phyllis a little. Largo added, "It was okay. So I know the two of you are playing Mrs. Newsom and Mrs. Wilbarger, and you were supposed to find a body in the dogtrot dressed up like a scarecrow."

If Eve had been here, she probably would

have corrected Largo and pointed out that Melissa and Julie were playing Peggy Nelson and Catherine Whittington, respectively, but that wasn't really relevant and it was likely a good thing Eve wasn't part of the conversation right now, Phyllis decided.

"That's right," Melissa said. "I was supposed to adjust the way the scarecrow is sitting, and then it topples over and we realize it's a body. Only . . ." She had to stop and take a deep breath. "Only as soon as I touched it, I could tell something was wrong. It wasn't a prop, like it was supposed to be. In fact it was . . . warm. So I looked closer . . ."

This time when she couldn't go on, it took several deep breaths before she could speak again.

"I looked closer, and I realized that it was really Lawrence Fremont."

"The director of the movie?"

"Yes. He had make-up on and straw under the hat and around his face to make him look like a scarecrow, but it was him. And his face was so . . . so twisted up that I knew right away something was wrong. I could tell . . . he was dead." Melissa shook her head and sniffled. "And after that, I know I started screaming and I fell down somehow, but really, the details are pretty fuzzy. I didn't start thinking clearly again until Earl was holding me and patting me on the back and telling me that everything was going to be all right."

"You *knew* Fremont was dead," Detective Largo repeated. "How did you know that? Did you see any blood? Were there any wounds?"

Melissa shook her head. "No, nothing like that that I could see. It was more a matter of . . . I'm sure you've been to funerals, Detective. You can tell somebody is dead by looking at their face."

Largo grunted and said, "Not always. But I'll give you that, Ms. Keller. After all that happened, did you see anything else? Anything that might give you an idea of *how* Fremont died?"

"I'm afraid not."

"Do you know why he was dressed as a scarecrow and sitting there on the hay bales in the dogtrot? You weren't expecting that, were you?"

"Good Lord, no! Lawrence was supposed to be directing that scene, not appearing in it. He's not like Alfred Hitchcock, you know."

Largo frowned, and Phyllis could tell she was puzzled by the comment.

Melissa must have picked up on that, too,

because she added, "Lawrence doesn't make cameos in his pictures, the way Hitchcock did."

"Oh." Largo shrugged. "Before my time. Do you know anybody who would have a reason to want Fremont dead?"

Phyllis was curious to hear what Melissa was going to say. Right offhand, she could think of several people who had had trouble with Lawrence Fremont. Were any of those problems big enough to drive someone to murder? They didn't seem so to Phyllis, but she knew from experience, it was impossible to tell from outside just how big a person's problems seemed to them . . . or what lengths they would go to in order to end them.

"No, I can't think of anyone," Melissa said. "Lawrence didn't always get along with everybody, you'll find that out pretty quickly if you question the people involved with making this movie, but there are *always* backstage squabbles on any picture. He could be an ass, but he didn't deserve to die for it."

"So he was an ass," Largo mused. She went on in a brisk tone, "If you think of anything else, call me." She handed Melissa a business card. "Oh, and don't leave town."

"You'll have to talk to Alan about that.

He's the producer."

"And I'm the detective investigating this case," Largo snapped. "You can go back and join your friends, but don't discuss the case with them."

Melissa nodded and went around the cabin. Largo turned to Phyllis and said, "As long as you're here, I might as well go ahead and ask you what you saw."

"Nothing that Ms. Keller hasn't already told you," Phyllis said. "We were sitting up there at that picnic table, where you saw us when you got here, and from there all I could tell was that something had frightened her. I saw her trip and fall and heard her screaming, but that's all I know."

The detective's eyes narrowed in thought. "Could you see that scarecrow from where you were?"

"Only the top of its head."

"How did it get there?"

Phyllis had to shake her head. "I don't know. It wasn't there earlier, and then it was. We were eating lunch, so I wasn't really paying attention. I assumed it was a prop and that someone from the prop department put it there on the hay bales. That's what would normally happen, I guess."

"It wouldn't be easy handling an actual body dressed like a scarecrow and getting it in place . . . but it happened before, didn't it?"

"No one was around when that happened," Phyllis reminded her. "Today there were dozens of people all over the place."

"Yeah, but who would have been paying attention to somebody dragging a prop around? You know how it is in any crowd. If you're carrying a clipboard, or if you just act like you're supposed to be doing whatever it is you're doing, most people don't pay any attention to you. You might as well be invisible."

For the moment, it seemed that Detective Largo had gotten over her resentment of Phyllis being involved in this case. She was talking to Phyllis more like they were fellow investigators. Phyllis didn't expect that to last, but for now she was glad not to be the object of the woman's hostility.

"Just out of curiosity, were all five of you up there at that picnic table where I saw you earlier?"

"You mean when Melissa discovered the body? No, Carolyn, Eve, and I were, but Ronnie and Sam were down by the old wagon." Phyllis pointed out the antique vehicle. "They were just as far away and had an even worse view than we did, so I don't imagine there's anything they could tell you."

"Ronnie?"

"Sam's granddaughter. She came to live with us this past summer."

Largo nodded. "They had a different angle on things. That means they might have seen something you didn't. Somebody will talk to them." She nodded briskly. "That's all for now. Don't leave the park until you've all been interviewed."

"I didn't intend to," Phyllis said.

Largo narrowed her eyes at that, but she didn't say anything. Phyllis walked back around the cabin to rejoin the others.

She wasn't the only one. Melissa was standing there with them as well. The streaks on her face had faded even more. She was starting to look more like herself, now that she had gotten over the shock of finding Lawrence Fremont's body.

"Have you solved the case yet?" Melissa asked as Phyllis walked up.

"What? No. I have no idea what happened to Mr. Fremont. We don't even know at this point if he was murdered."

Carolyn said, "Who dresses a corpse that died of natural causes in a scarecrow outfit and props them up like that? It was murder, Phyllis, and you know it."

"What I'm wondering about is *how* he was killed," Melissa said. "Like I told that detective, I didn't see a mark on him."

"Poison," Carolyn said with an emphatic nod. "I'll bet it was poison. It has been before, you know."

Melissa also nodded and said, "It has, hasn't it?"

Phyllis felt a little as if she had plunged down a rabbit hole. She said, "Why did you want me there while the detective questioned you?"

"Because like I told her, you're going to be the one to solve this," Melissa answered as if that were the simplest, most obvious thing in the world. "No killer can get away with something like this while you're around."

"I think you've got an inflated opinion of my capabilities."

"Not at all," Melissa insisted. "I studied you for weeks, Phyllis, before we started shooting. I know what you can do. I feel like I know you about as well as I know myself. In fact . . ." Her eyes lit up as an idea occurred to her. "I'm going to help you. Phyllis Newsom and Peggy Nelson are going to team up to solve this murder!"

CHAPTER 13

Phyllis stared at her for a long moment before she was able to say, "That's the craziest thing I've ever heard!" She was so surprised she didn't even preface that with a comment about not intending to give any offense.

"No, it's not," Melissa said. "I know your methods, Phyllis. I think I've even got a pretty good idea how your mind works. When you're playing somebody based on a real person, that's what you have to do, you know. You have to burrow right into them and learn what makes them tick."

Phyllis didn't like the idea of being burrowed into, and she thought Melissa was getting carried away. It might be a good idea to deflect this now, while she still could.

"There's really no point in thinking about it," she said as she shook her head. "Detective Largo won't like it if I try to interfere in her case. I'm sure I won't have anything to do with the investigation."

"That never stopped you before, did it? The cops got their noses out of joint every time you started poking around in some murder, but you did it anyway."

Carolyn said, "Phyllis always had a good reason for doing that. I was accused of killing someone, or Eve was, or someone else we knew. And every time, Phyllis was convinced the person was innocent and knew the police would railroad them into a conviction."

"I don't think the police would railroad anyone —" Phyllis began.

"The district attorney would," Carolyn responded with a contemptuous snort. "We've seen plenty of evidence of that over the years."

Phyllis couldn't deny anything her friend was saying. On numerous occasions, she'd felt like she *had* to get involved in a case in order to prevent a miscarriage of justice. She had no such motivation here, though.

"Let's not get ahead of ourselves here," she told the others. "Detective Largo may find a witness who can clear up the whole thing. There may be enough physical evidence to solve the case. Let's just wait and see."

Ronnie said, "Here come the CSI guys."

She was right. A crew of crime scene techs had arrived at the park and were soon set up, scouring the dogtrot and the area around the cabin for evidence . . . including the corpse. The medical examiner arrived shortly thereafter, although he wouldn't be able to get started on his grim task until the technicians were finished with theirs.

Meanwhile, Detective Largo was questioning Julie Cordell. Phyllis and her friends sat down at one of the tables and watched as the police detective talked one by one with Julie, Heidi Lancaster, Robert Harkness, Alan Sammons, and Earl Thorpe.

"I don't see those writers anywhere," Carolyn commented. "Isn't she going to interview them, too?"

"Writers always get talked to last, and usually by some flunky," Eve said. "I'm sure Detective Largo will have another officer talk to Jason and Deanne."

Eve was probably right, but Phyllis still wondered where the screenwriters were. She saw Becca Peterson standing with some other members of the supporting cast. Should she have mentioned to Detective Largo what she had heard about Becca and Fremont? Largo hadn't actually asked *her* if she knew of anyone with a reason to want the director dead, only Melissa, and Phyllis hadn't volunteered the information. Maybe she would, depending on how things played out with the case, but for now, Becca seemed more like a victim to her, and she didn't want to cause unnecessary trouble for the young woman.

A familiar stocky figure emerged from a newly arrived vehicle in the parking lot and started along one of the concrete paths. The man saw Phyllis and the others and detoured over to the picnic table.

"Why do I get this unmistakable feeling of déjà vu?" Chief Ralph Whitmire asked. "How are you, Mrs. Newsom?"

"Better this time than last, Chief," Phyllis answered honestly. "I'm not the one who found the body."

"But there really *is* a body?"

"Oh, yes. Lawrence Fremont, the director of the movie that was shooting here today."

Whitmire sighed. "When I heard that people from Hollywood were going to be making a movie out of Ms. Turner's book, the craziest thought crossed my mind."

"That there might be a murder?" Carolyn asked.

"Well, yes. I told myself that would never happen, though. Clearly, I was wrong."

"It hasn't been ruled a homicide yet," Phyllis pointed out. "The medical examiner hasn't even gotten close to the body."

Whitmire cocked his head in acknowledgment of that, but he didn't appear convinced. Phyllis couldn't blame him for thinking the worst. That was an occupational hazard.

"I'll go see what Detective Largo has found out so far," the chief said. "And I'll try to soothe any ruffled feathers those Hollywood bigwigs have."

Carolyn said, "One of those Hollywood bigwigs might be a murderer."

"Yeah, I know."

As Whitmire walked toward the crime scene, Phyllis thought about what Carolyn had just said. In all likelihood, one of the members of the movie company *was* the murderer, assuming that Lawrence Fremont had been murdered. It was just too farfetched to think that someone local would have had a reason to kill the director, especially under such bizarre circumstances. The visitors from Hollywood hadn't even had all that much interaction with the citizens of Weatherford. The likelihood of one of them having a grudge worthy of murder was almost non-existent.

Almost, Phyllis told herself . . . but in a murder investigation, it didn't pay to rule out anything too soon.

Gradually, the crowd in the park began to thin out. People were questioned and released once the police had their contact information.

"Oh, look there!" Ronnie exclaimed. "The cops have got that guy in handcuffs."

It was true. Two officers were leading away a glum-looking man in his thirties. Phyllis had never seen him before, at least that she could recall.

"Do you think he's the murderer?" Ronnie went on.

"That's not likely," Carolyn said. "Chief Whitmire and Detective Largo are still down there by the log cabin talking to the movie people."

"And it looks like the medical examiner is just starting to examine the body," Eve added.

Phyllis said, "It's more likely that man had an outstanding warrant and was taken into custody when he identified himself."

"But I saw that guy earlier," Ronnie said. "He was one of the extras, like Granddad and me. Are you seriously saying that somebody who's wanted by the cops would risk getting arrested by showing up to be in a movie?"

Sam grinned and said, "The lure of fame and fortune is overwhelmin'. Wouldn't surprise me if they picked up more than one fella here today who's been dodgin' a warrant."

"You're probably right, but I think if I was wanted by the law, I'd be more careful than that."

"Just don't ever do anything you'd have to go on the lam from," Sam advised.

"Yeah, I'll try not to," Ronnie said dryly.

Eve was right about the medical examiner. The crime scene techs had finished their work. The two ambulance attendants who had accompanied the ME to the scene moved the body, laying it out on a couple of hay bales for a preliminary examination. Phyllis was glad she and the others were sitting far enough away that they couldn't see any details.

The medical examiner didn't take long. The attendants lifted the corpse and moved it into a body bag on a gurney sitting in the dogtrot. One of them zipped the bag closed, then they rolled the gurney along one of the walkways toward the parking lot.

"Will they take the crime scene tape down so the festival can go on tomorrow?" Ronnie asked.

"Would people still come when a murder's been committed here?" Melissa asked.

"You'd be surprised," Carolyn said.

"Death brings notoriety with it, and most people have a morbid streak. They want to see where something happened, even if it's something bad."

Melissa nodded and said, "Of course, I ought to know that. People still drive around Hollywood looking for the graves of movie stars, and they flock to places where famous crimes took place."

"You know what Mencken said about nobody ever goin' broke underestimatin' the taste of the American public," Sam said. "If the cops let 'em go ahead with the festival, the park'll be full of people again, mark my words on that."

"I hope they do," Carolyn said. "Murder or no murder, the more we can help out people who are going hungry, the better."

No one could argue with that.

As Detective Largo finished questioning them, the others involved in the movie drifted over to the table. Those already sitting there scooted over to make room on the benches. Julie was first, then Heidi Lancaster and Robert Harkness. Phyllis noted that Harkness was careful to sit on the other side and at the other end of the table from Melissa. She wondered why such animosity existed between them. Harkness seemed like a decent, friendly fellow, and

Melissa, despite her crazy idea about her and Phyllis investigating Lawrence Fremont's murder, had been very sweet and down to earth so far.

Julie said, "That detective warned us not to discuss the case. We're not going to abide by that, are we?"

"We've already been talking about it," Melissa said. "Who do you think could have done it?"

Julie shook her head. "I don't have any idea. Lawrence rubbed people the wrong way a lot of the time, but I don't know anybody who actually hated him enough to kill him."

"Becca might have," Harkness said.

Julie snapped an angry look at him. "What do you mean by that?"

"I mean I've heard rumors about the two of them."

"Oh, shoot, there are always rumors about everybody," Melissa said. "You can't put much stock in them. You probably wouldn't know it, since you come from Australia and haven't been working over here all that long, but the gossip about Lawrence goes back years. Decades even."

Carolyn said, "That's what I don't understand. Every time there's some new scandal about a producer or a director or somebody like that abusing his position of power, it turns out people were aware of it for a long time. Why didn't anyone speak up before now?"

"Because it's a bottom-line business," Melissa said. "And as long as the bottom-line is healthy, people are reluctant to rock the boat." She shrugged. "And there's a certain sense that, well, that's just the way things are. The way they've always been. I'm not saying it's right, but . . ."

"Folks have a hard time goin' against tradition," Sam said, "even when it's a bad tradition."

"Exactly."

Julie glared at Harkness and said, "Don't go around spreading rumors about Becca. She's a nice girl."

The actor held up his hands defensively. "I didn't mean anything. And I didn't even mention her name to that police detective."

"Fine," Julie said with a curt nod.

Phyllis had taken note of the way Julie leaped to Becca Peterson's defense. That struck her as a little odd. Maybe Julie and Becca were friends, although nothing had been said about that so far.

A commotion over by the stone building that contained the restrooms drew Phyllis's attention then. Two uniformed officers headed toward the log cabin, and between them was Jason Wilkes. Each of the officers held one of Jason's arms as if to keep him from getting away. As they came closer, though, Phyllis got the impression that it was more a case of hanging on to him to make sure he didn't fall down.

"There's Jason," Eve said, having seen the same thing as Phyllis. "Oh, dear, he doesn't look good."

The others turned in that direction, and Harkness said, "I believe the poor fellow's as drunk as a skunk."

That was Phyllis's assessment, too. Jason's stumbling gait, red face, and general air of dishevelment made it pretty obvious. She wondered if he had been holed up in the restroom, drinking, ever since the confrontation with Lawrence Fremont that morning. Earlier, Deanne hadn't known where he was, and that would explain his disappearance.

The officers brought Jason to where Chief Whitmire and Detective Largo were standing. When they let go of him, he swayed and they had to grab hold again. Largo made a face and shook her head. She pointed to one of the nearby tables. The officers marched Jason over there and sat him down. Slowly, he leaned forward until his head rested on the concrete table.

"Well, Jason's accounted for," Melissa said, "but we still don't know where Deanne is, do we?"

"We talked to her earlier," Eve said. "I haven't seen her since then, though."

Alan Sammons and Earl Thorpe trudged over to the table to join them. Sammons said, "The detective says that we're all free to go, for now. We won't be doing any more shooting today, that's for sure."

"Are you suspending the picture, Alan?" Melissa asked.

Sammons shook his head. "No, not yet. I'm still hoping we can salvage something." He laughed, but it was a humorless sound. "To be honest, I can't afford to shut down production. What a mess. Can't afford to stop, can't afford to go on. But we will, somehow."

Thorpe said, "The park will still be decked out for the festival when it's over, won't it? Maybe we can get the shots we still need afterward. We got quite a bit of crowd footage in the can already, so we wouldn't need a *lot* of extras, just a handful. Most of what was left to shoot was with the principals."

Sammons rubbed his chin and frowned in thought. "Maybe . . . if the city will allow us to come back and shoot, say, day after tomorrow or even next week. I don't think the cops are going to let us leave right away, so we might as well put the time to good use." He nodded decisively. "Earl, you'll take over for now. Is that all right with you?"

"Whatever it takes to save the picture," Thorpe said.

Sammons looked around at the cast members. "Any objections?"

"Not from me," Melissa said, and the others shook their heads.

"It's settled, then. As soon as we can work out the details, we'll shoot the other scenes we need to do here, then head back down to Austin to wrap up the rest of the picture. I'll need to make some calls . . . and of course some of this depends on what the cops will let us do . . ." Sammons drew in a deep breath and added, "For the sake of this picture and all of us, we'd better hope that old saying is right."

"What old saying?" Harkness asked.

"The one about there being no such thing as bad publicity!"

CHAPTER 14

Since Isabel Largo had said it was all right for them to leave, Phyllis and the others stood up and got ready to head for the parking lot. As they did, it occurred to Phyllis that she hadn't retrieved her pie plate from the craft services table.

"You two can go on to the car," she told Carolyn and Eve. "I'll be there in a minute." Sam and Ronnie would go back to the house in Sam's pickup, of course.

She walked toward the portable tables where the food had been set out, but before she got there she saw that crime scene tape had been strung up around them and a uniformed officer was standing outside the tape, keeping an eye on things. He noticed her coming in that direction and asked, "Can I help you with something, ma'am?"

Phyllis studied the tables. Some of the food still remained, mostly fruit. The rest had been eaten at lunch. She could see her pie plate at the end of the table where she had left it. The cover had been removed, and the plate was empty now except for some crumbs of crust that remained.

"That's my plate —" she began, pointing at it.

The officer held up a hand to stop her. "Sorry, ma'am, it'll have to stay there for now. Detective Largo says that everything on these tables is considered evidence. I'm sure you'll be able to get it back sooner or later."

As soon as she had seen the crime scene tape, Phyllis had thought the same thing about evidence. And that told her something.

The food wouldn't be important unless the police suspected Lawrence Fremont had been poisoned. Melissa had said that she hadn't seen any blood or wounds on Fremont's body, so if he hadn't died of natural causes, poisoning was the most logical conclusion.

Clearly her pie had been a success, Phyllis thought, since it was all gone. Under the circumstances, though, that was scant comfort.

"Thank you," she said to the officer, then turned and walked toward the parking lot. It was just a pie plate, after all, she told herself. If she never got it back, it wouldn't matter.

"Problem?" Carolyn asked when Phyllis got into the Lincoln and shut the door.

"No, I just went to get that pie plate and container. But the police are going to impound everything that was on those tables as evidence, I guess."

"Of course! That man was poisoned, just like I said."

"Maybe," Phyllis said as she turned the key in the ignition. As she backed out, she saw the crime scene van parked next to one of the motor homes across the road. That would be the one occupied by Lawrence Fremont, she thought. The technicians were probably in there combing through it for evidence, too.

Sam's pickup pulled into the driveway before the garage door finished lowering behind the Lincoln. Phyllis caught sight of it in the rearview mirror and pushed the button on the remote control to stop the door's descent. Another push raised it again.

Sam and Ronnie joined them in the garage. As they went into the house, Ronnie said, "I'll bet all my friends have heard about what happened, but I'm gonna post some pictures anyway." She was already

164

poking at her phone's screen as she went through the kitchen.

"I don't know about the rest of you," Carolyn said, "but I could use some coffee."

"Sounds good to me," Sam said.

The other three sat down at the table while Carolyn started the coffee brewing. Phyllis said, "I never noticed, did the police question all of you as well?"

"Yeah, while you were talkin' to Detective Largo and Ms. Keller," Sam said. "One of the uniforms did it."

"There wasn't anything we could tell him, though," Eve said. "Just the same thing you did, I'm sure, Phyllis. And then he took our names and numbers."

Carolyn pulled out the other chair and sat down. "You're going to have to write a book about this, Eve. A novel about a murder committed during the making of a movie based on a novel about a murder that was committed in real life —"

"Stop," Eve said, putting her hands to her head. "I'm getting dizzy!"

"Art imitates life," Sam said. "Or is it the other way around? This is startin' to remind me of that scene in *Citizen Kane* where Orson Welles walks in front of the mirror and you see dozens of him fadin' away into infinity."

"Does that mean the murder cases are never going to end?" Carolyn asked.

"I hope that's not the way it is," Phyllis said with a fervent sigh. "Did Ronnie enjoy the day, at least before everything that happened this afternoon?"

Sam nodded and said, "She sure seemed like it. You know she said that about maybe gettin' involved with some little theater group and takin' drama in college. She mentioned the same thing to me before she said it to y'all. It's good to see her excited about something. She never has really talked much about what her plans are for the future. Maybe she'll be a famous actress."

"I'm not sure that's something I'd encourage," Carolyn said. "I mean, these Hollywood people *seem* nice right now, but the place has been known as a . . . a den of debauchery for a hundred years now! I'm sure a lot of that image is overblown, but Hollywood never would have gotten such a reputation if there wasn't *some* truth to all the sordid gossip."

"Some people believe that all writers are degenerates, too, you know," Eve said.

Carolyn just shrugged.

Phyllis said, "Ronnie's still young enough that she'll probably change her mind a

166

dozen times about what she wants to do with her life. It's too soon to worry about that."

The four of them had just gotten their coffee and settled down around the table again when the doorbell rang. Phyllis wasn't expecting anyone, but she stood up and said, "I'll see who it is. No need for the rest of you to get up."

She walked down the hall, past the living room, into the foyer. Through the narrow window at the side of the door, she saw a nondescript sedan parked at the curb in front of the house. When she leaned to the side, she could see who was standing on the porch.

Detective Isabel Largo.

Phyllis's first thought was that there had been a break in the case. Would the detective stop by to tell her about that if it was true? Possibly. Despite the momentary irritation Largo had displayed when she found out that Phyllis was involved, the two of them had been on reasonably good terms in the past. Later, after Largo had questioned Melissa Keller, she had seemed almost friendly. Phyllis hoped the detective was here to deliver some good news.

But of course, there was only one way to find out.

She opened the door and said, "Hello, Detective. Won't you —"

Phyllis fell silent when Largo held up the thing she was holding and asked, "Is this yours, Mrs. Newsom?"

It was Phyllis's pie plate — or at least a pie plate that *looked* like the same one — sealed up in a large, clear evidence bag.

Phyllis drew in a sharp breath. She hadn't expected to get the plate back quite this soon . . . and she certainly didn't believe that Detective Largo had driven all the way over here just to give it back to her. That meant the plate was important for some other reason, and Phyllis could think of only one thing that could be.

She remained calm, though, as she said, "Is there a piece of masking tape stuck to the bottom of it?"

Largo turned the bag so Phyllis could see the tape through it. "Yes. Looks like there was some writing on it at one time, but it seems to have worn off."

"That's because I put the tape on there and wrote my name on it a couple of months ago when I took a pie to a potluck dinner at church," Phyllis explained. "I hadn't gotten around to pulling the tape off since then." She made a face. "It always leaves a little sticky stuff, and you have to use special cleaner to get it off . . . But you don't care about that, do you, Detective?"

"What kind of pie was in it?"

Instead of answering directly, Phyllis said, "Please, come on in. We might as well have this conversation in the living room, instead of you having to stand out there on the porch."

Largo hesitated for a moment, then said, "Sure, why not?" She walked into the house and Phyllis closed the door behind her.

Sam, Carolyn, and Eve appeared at the far end of the hall. Sam said, "We figured we'd better come see what was goin' on. Hello, Detective. Want a cup of coffee?"

"No, I —" Largo stopped short, then went on, "Actually, that sounds good. Thank you."

"I'll bring it," Sam said. "And yours, too, Phyllis."

"We were just sitting and talking in the kitchen," Phyllis explained to the detective.

"About Lawrence Fremont's murder, I'm sure."

"Then you've determined that his death was a homicide?" Eve asked.

"Phyllis, is that your pie plate?" Carolyn said.

"Let's all go in the living room and sit down," Phyllis suggested. "Then Detective

Largo can tell us why she's here."

It wasn't going to be anything good, though, Phyllis was already sure of that.

Sam came back from the kitchen with a fresh cup of coffee for Largo, as well as Phyllis's cup, and when he handed it to her he said, "I topped it off for you."

"Thank you. Please, Detective, have a seat."

They all sat down, with Largo taking one of the straight-backed chairs and sitting forward on it as if she couldn't quite bring herself to relax. She placed the evidence bag containing Phyllis's pie plate on a small round table beside her. Phyllis couldn't help but be aware that a piece of evidence in a murder case was sitting on an old-fashioned lace doily that her own mother had made many decades earlier.

Detective Largo sipped the coffee, then said, "I really shouldn't be here."

"You came to ask me to identify that pie plate," Phyllis said. "That falls within your duty, doesn't it?"

"Sure, but getting you to ID the plate doesn't mean I ought to come in and sit down and drink coffee like a friend."

Phyllis smiled. "I don't think we're enemies."

"No," Largo said, shaking her head

slightly. "I don't think so, either. By the way, I also have the plastic container this plate was in bagged up out in the car. It'll be evidence, too."

"Evidence of what?" Carolyn asked.

"Murder, Mrs. Wilbarger, just as you thought." The detective looked around at them. "Lawrence Fremont was poisoned. Cyanide. The medical examiner found it in his stomach."

"The autopsy is already done?" Phyllis asked, surprised. "That was fast."

"It's not every day an award-winning Hollywood director is killed in Weatherford. The medical examiner's putting a rush on it. The autopsy's still going on, but the ME stopped and called me as soon as he determined for sure that Fremont was poisoned. He found something else in the stomach, too."

Phyllis took a deep breath and said, "Let me guess. Pecan pie."

"That's right." Largo looked at the plate on the table beside her. "As far as we've been able to determine, the only pecan pie anywhere in the park today was the one that you brought with you, Mrs. Newsom."

"That's insane!" Carolyn burst out. "You can't honestly believe Phyllis poisoned that man. None of us had even met him until

171

last night. Why in the world would she do such a thing?"

"I never said that she did," Largo responded coolly. "For what it's worth, Mrs. Newsom, the idea that you killed Fremont never crossed my mind."

"It is worth something," Phyllis said, "and it's always good to hear." Her brain was working quickly. "Was there anything else in Mr. Fremont's stomach?"

Largo shook her head. "Not according to the ME. And since it's unlikely Fremont ate cyanide by itself, it's pretty certain it was in the pie. The sweet taste could have concealed it nicely. What I have to find out is how it got there, because I know good and well it wasn't an accident."

"No, it wouldn't have been."

Carolyn said, "It wasn't there when the pie left the house this morning."

"So, just for the record, how *did* the pie get to the park?" Largo asked. "You put it in that container and carried it there yourself, Mrs. Newsom?"

"Yes, it was in the back seat of my car, and then when we got there I took it into the park. We ran into Mr. Sammons, and he took it and gave it to —"

"Gave it to who?" Largo asked. "Why did you stop that way?"

"I just don't want to seem like I'm pointing the finger at anyone," Phyllis said. With Largo's intent gaze boring in on her, she knew she had to answer. "Mr. Sammons gave the pie to a production assistant, a young woman he called Teddy. He told her to take it and put it on one of the craft services tables. He said she should put a note on it telling everyone to keep their hands off for the time being. He knew that Mr. Fremont liked the pie he had here last night and would be upset if this one was finished off before he got a chance at it."

"Teddy Demming," Largo said. "I questioned her, but I don't recall her saying anything about the pie."

"But you wouldn't have known to ask her about it at that point, and she was so busy, running errands all over the park all day, that she'd probably forgotten about it by then."

"I don't think she would have forgotten about it if she doctored it up with cyanide. Do you know of any reason she would have a grudge against Fremont?"

Phyllis shook her head. "I never saw her until today and still haven't actually met her. So I have no idea."

Largo looked around at the others, who all shook their heads.

Phyllis recalled the harsh way Fremont had spoken to Teddy that morning, but as it turned out, the director had been angry at Jason and Deanne Wilkes, not at Teddy herself. That wouldn't rise to the level of a murder motive.

But then she thought about the solicitous way Teddy had spoken to Jason and touched his arm. Maybe there was nothing between them . . . maybe Teddy had just been commiserating with the screenwriter . . . but if they *were* involved, could Fremont's treatment of Jason have angered Teddy enough to strike back?

"Just because Teddy put the pie on the table doesn't mean she did anything to it," Phyllis said. "With the crowd and all the confusion, there's no telling what someone might have done."

"The container had a hands-off sign on it."

"That wouldn't have stopped anyone from opening it for a moment and then closing it up again."

"That's true," Largo admitted. "In a madhouse like that, nobody's got a concrete alibi." She frowned. "How could the killer be sure Fremont would get the poison and not somebody else?"

Sam said, "Nobody else has dropped

174

dead, have they?"

"Not that I've heard about. And I think that under the circumstances, I would have heard. So the whole pie wasn't poisoned . . . just the part that Lawrence Fremont ate."

Phyllis nodded and said, "That's the way it seems to me."

"None of this explains why he was dressed like a scarecrow," Eve said. "Or how he got there on those hay bales in the dogtrot."

Largo grimaced and said, "Yeah, poison's one thing, but all that other crazy stuff . . ." She shook her head. "We'll figure it out, though." She drank more of the coffee and then stood up, reaching for the pie plate in the evidence bag. "I'll have to take this with me, but I'll try to see to it that you do get it back, sooner or later."

"I'm not worried about that," Phyllis assured her. "It's more important to find out who killed Mr. Fremont."

Detective Largo looked at her and asked, "Did you like the guy, Mrs. Newsom?"

"No," Phyllis answered honestly. "I don't believe any of us did."

"Not particularly," Carolyn agreed.

"But whether we did or not, his killer shouldn't get away with it."

"Yeah, we're on the same page about that. Thanks for the coffee, and for letting me chew this over some."

"Anything we can do to help, Detective, just let us know."

Largo nodded, smiled faintly, and let herself out the front door. Phyllis followed her and closed it behind her.

"Hey," Ronnie said from halfway down the stairs where she had come to a stop, "was that that lady cop?"

"Detective Largo," Phyllis said. "Yes, it was."

"Did she ask you to help her solve the case?"

"No, of course not." Phyllis debated how much to tell the teenager about the case, but she knew Ronnie would get all of the information out of Sam, anyway. "It appears that Mr. Fremont was poisoned . . . and that someone put the poison in that pecan pie I took to the park today."

Ronnie's eyes got huge. "You mean you provided the murder weapon?"

"Well, I wouldn't put it like . . ." Phyllis made a face. "Yes, I suppose I did."

Ronnie turned around. "I've got to post —"

"Hold on there, young lady," Sam said. He had come up beside Phyllis in time to hear the exchange. "That information is part of the police investigation. You go postin' it on-line, you're liable to get Detective Largo in all sorts of trouble, and probably Phyllis, too. You need to keep it to yourself for now, even though I know you kids like to share everything."

"But this is a great story, Granddad —"

"I want your word," Sam said flatly.

Ronnie sighed. "Okay. I won't post any more than I already have. I give you my word."

"I'm obliged to you for that."

Before Ronnie could say anything else, the doorbell rang again. As Phyllis turned toward the door, she didn't expect it to be anything good waiting for her.

When she opened the door, though, her son Mike was standing there on the porch.

CHAPTER 15

"I heard about what happened at the park, Mom," Mike said. "Are you okay?"

"Yes, of course. Why wouldn't I be?" Phyllis stepped back. "Come on in."

Mike wore his sheriff's department uniform and had his hat in one hand. As he stepped into the foyer and Phyllis closed the door, he said, "I just finished my shift. I wanted to come over here earlier, but I couldn't until now. As soon as I heard that somebody had been murdered at the park, and that the body was dressed like a scarecrow, I knew that you . . ."

He looked a little sheepish as his voice trailed off. Phyllis said, "You knew I'd be right in the middle of the case, isn't that what you were about to say?"

"Well, yeah. I mean . . . you've got to admit, something that bizarre happening in Weatherford . . ."

Carolyn said, "It's just like that other time,

right down to the fact that the victim was poisoned."

Mike's eyebrows rose. "He was? I hadn't heard that part of it yet."

"Detective Largo was just here," Phyllis said.

"Isabel? She gave you details on an active investigation? I'm a little surprised she'd do that. She's usually pretty by-the-book."

Phyllis knew that Mike and Isabel Largo were friends. She had wondered occasionally if they were a little *too* friendly, since Mike was married to a wonderful woman and he and his wife Sarah had a beautiful little boy, Phyllis's grandson Bobby.

Every time that thought crossed her mind, though, she scolded herself for such an old-fashioned, judgmental attitude. It was entirely possible for a man and a woman to be good friends without anything else going on. Such things just hadn't been as common when she was younger.

Phyllis put a hand on Mike's arm and said, "Come on in and sit down. I'll tell you all about it."

"Want some coffee, Mike?" Sam asked.

"Sure. That'd be great."

Phyllis hoped that Detective Largo wouldn't mind her sharing what she had learned with Mike. He had provided her

179

with inside information and helped her solve several cases in the past, and she knew that he could be trusted absolutely. Once they were all settled in the living room, Phyllis spent a few minutes filling him in on everything that had happened today.

Once she had finished, Mike said with a grim note in his voice, "I'm glad you weren't the one to find the body this time. That's happened too often already."

"I certainly can't argue with that. We were pretty close by, though. Still, I didn't have to look right into that man's face, like poor Melissa did. That was a terrible shock to her."

Mike sat back in an armchair and cocked his right ankle on his left knee. "From the sound of it, somebody could have gotten a piece of that pie, doped it with the poison, and given it to this guy Fremont. Would he have just gobbled it down without noticing something was wrong with it?"

"Cyanide isn't completely tasteless," Phyllis said, "but it blends in well with something sweet and might not be noticeable right away. He really liked the piece he had here last night. The recipe was the same, so I think it's feasible that he might have done that. I've been thinking about it, and that's the only sequence of events that explains how someone would be able to poison Mr. Fremont without taking the risk of killing other people, too."

"So where was he when this happened?"

Phyllis shook her head. "Right now, there's no way of knowing. He dropped out of sight for a while around the middle of the day. He may have been in the motor home he was using."

"The crime scene boys were goin' over it," Sam added. "We don't know what they might've found."

"I might be able to find out later." Mike looked at Phyllis. "But do I need to? I mean, you're not investigating this murder, right? You don't have any reason to get any more involved than you already are?"

"Not that I can think of." Phyllis paused, then went on, "Although Melissa Keller seems to think that she and I should work together to solve it."

Mike's eyebrows rose. "The actress who's playing you?"

"Peggy Nelson," Eve said. "The character's not actually Phyllis."

Ignoring that, Phyllis went on, "I didn't agree to do that, though. Melissa's nice, but because she's studied the things I've done to help her play the part, she has this crazy idea about playing detective instead —"

181

"She might be able to help. She knows all the people involved."

Mike's comment surprised Phyllis. In the past, except on rare occasions, he had always warned her not to get involved in murder cases and had tried to discourage her investigations. Now he almost seemed to be saying that he thought it would be a good thing if she and Melissa tried to find the killer.

"I'm hoping that Detective Largo clears the case quickly," she said. "Then Melissa can go back to making movies and I can go on with my life . . . which is just fine without any murders, I might add."

"Well, sure, that would be best." Mike drank the last of his coffee and stood up. "I'd better be getting on home. I called Sarah and told her I was stopping by here, but I don't want her to worry. Now that I know you're okay . . ." He looked around the room at the others. "And that nobody here is in any danger of being arrested —"

"It's not like we make a habit of being murder suspects," Carolyn said with a sniff.

Mike laughed. "No, but you've got to admit, it *has* come up from time to time. I'm just glad you're all on the sidelines of this one. Maybe it'll stay that way." He came over to the sofa where Phyllis was sitting with Sam, bent to give her a quick hug, and said, "See you later."

They all stayed where they were as Mike let himself out. When he was gone, Carolyn said, "I'm going to call the other members on the board of the food pantry and find out if they've heard anything about whether the festival will go on as planned tomorrow."

She left the room to do that. Sam frowned in thought for a moment and said to Phyllis, "If they do have the festival, are you still gonna enter that pie contest? I mean . . ."

"After my pie was used as a weapon to help murder someone?" Phyllis shuddered. "My goodness, I hadn't even thought about that! I don't think I could bake another pecan pie, I'm sure of that much, anyway."

"Well, it's a good thing there are lots of different kinds of pies in the world, then."

"I suppose so." Despite everything that had happened, Sam's question made the wheels of Phyllis's brain start to turn over as she considered what sort of pie might be a viable option for the contest. Old habits were hard to break, she supposed, especially competitive ones, and after a minute or so, she said, "You know, I do have a recipe for a spicy caramel apple pie that I've been thinking about trying."

"Sounds mighty good," Sam said. He managed not to lick his lips, but Phyllis could tell he was thinking about it.

It was that evening before a decision was reached between the food pantry's board of directors, the police department, and the city manager on whether the festival could continue as planned. Chief Ralph Whitmire had the final word, according to what Carolyn told the others. When he agreed that it wasn't necessary to keep the park and everything in it cordoned off as a crime scene, the decision was fairly easy.

The Harvest Festival would proceed.

"The chief is going to have extra officers on duty there during the day, though," Carolyn said, "because he expects an even larger crowd than usual. I feel a little bad about saying it, because I know it means some people will come because of the murder, but I hope he's right."

"The more folks show up, the more canned food will be collected," Sam said.

"That's right. So some good will come out of a terrible situation. It's all right to be pleased with that, isn't it?"

"I think so," Phyllis said.

Supper had been a quick affair. Carolyn chopped up some of the leftover brisket, added some barbeque sauce, and put it on baked potatoes. After they cleaned up the kitchen, the four of them had moved to the living room. Ronnie was upstairs in her room, probably posting something on her computer or phone. She went out casually with some of the boys she attended school with, but she didn't have a date tonight.

In a way, Phyllis was glad of that. She didn't think Weatherford was any more of a dangerous place than normal tonight because of Lawrence Fremont's murder. She was convinced that was an isolated incident. But it was still good to have everyone home and safe under one roof.

"Anybody feel like watchin' a movie?" Sam asked. "Would it be too creepy to stream one of Lawrence Fremont's films?"

"Yes," Carolyn answered without hesitation. "It would."

Phyllis said, "I don't even know what other movies he made. Do you mind if I look them up, Sam?"

"Shoot, no, go right ahead."

Carolyn got to her feet. "I think I'm going up to my room. This has been a very tiring day."

Phyllis couldn't argue with that, but at the same time, she felt oddly energized, as if she wasn't going to be able to relax for a while. She knew that was a result of her brain engaging with the mystery of Fremont's death, whether she wanted that to happen or not.

"I believe I'll say good night, too," Eve said. "I want to check my email . . . and I might do a little writing."

"A new book?" Carolyn said.

"Just some ideas."

"That Wilkes woman got you thinking, didn't she?"

"Maybe . . ."

They continued talking as they left the living room and headed upstairs. Phyllis went to the desk in the corner with the computer and monitor sitting on it and started searching for information on Lawrence Fremont. She had taken a cursory look at his film career when she found out that he was directing the movie based on Eve's book, but now she began digging deeper.

Lawrence Fremont, she discovered, actually came from a theater background. He had done some acting in New York as a young man, mostly in off-Broadway plays, but he had made it to Broadway a few times in supporting roles. Somewhere along the way he had gotten involved in directing and had started to carve out a reputation for himself, again mostly in off-Broadway productions.

Then he had landed a job directing a few episodes of a police procedural television series that was shot in New York and had parlayed that into more TV work, moving on to Los Angeles for that. He had been quite busy with TV in the second half of the Eighties, before directing his first film in 1990. That had been a low-budget independent picture, but it had gotten good reviews and had decent box office returns, for what it was. By the end of the Nineties, Fremont had been a well-respected director who had worked steadily.

Those were just the bare bones of his career, though. Phyllis looked for more about his personal life. It was possible someone could have had some purely mercenary reason for poisoning Fremont, but it seemed to her that anyone who used a murder method such as poison wanted the victim to suffer. That much hatred required a personal motive.

She went back to the early days of his career in New York, and after several minutes of searching that turned up innocuous stories on various theater websites, she found a mention of Fremont in a newspaper story about the suicide of a young actress who had leaped off a skyscraper to her death. Phyllis's eyes widened at that. The young woman had been a member of the cast of a play Fremont had directed. She had been engaged to an actor in the cast, but they had broken up recently and that was considered to be the reason she had taken her own life.

Had she ended her engagement because of Lawrence Fremont? Nothing in the story indicated that, but Phyllis had to ask herself the question.

She looked up the actress who had committed suicide, just in case there was a connection between her and the people involved in this movie. As far as Phyllis could tell, no such link existed. But she filed the facts away in her memory anyway.

There was nothing as dramatic as that in any of the other stories she could find about Fremont's theater career. He had been married to an actress in New York, but only for fourteen months before they divorced. Phyllis couldn't find anything suspicious about the woman. Apparently, she had retired from acting, married someone else, and now lived in New Jersey and worked as a real estate agent. A dead end, Phyllis decided.

Over the years, Fremont had been linked romantically with a number of other women, both in show business and out of it, but he never married again. Archived pages from gossip websites, newspapers, and tabloids hinted at various improprieties but wrote openly about Fremont's temper and the difficulties he had with different actors, crew members, and studio executives. He had gotten mixed up in several physical altercations when the victims of his wrath or his cruel practical jokes took violent exception to them. Most recently he had traded punches with . . .

Phyllis sat back and stared at the screen. Three movies back, Lawrence Fremont had gotten into a fight with an actor from Australia who was making his first American movie.

Robert Harkness.

Eagerly now, she read on. Harkness was taller and heavier than Fremont, but from the sound of it, the director knew how to handle himself in a fight. Both men had wound up bloody and battered. Harkness had finished the movie, though. Phyllis wondered if he and Fremont had patched up their differences. Harkness had been cast in this film, so it seemed that they must have. But maybe not. Maybe Harkness had been seething inside, just waiting for his chance to settle the old score . . .

Harkness didn't strike Phyllis as a poisoner, though. He would have been more likely to go after Fremont with his fists again. But that was just her impression, Phyllis reminded herself. She didn't know the man well enough to say anything for sure about him.

That discovery made her think that maybe she ought to check the casts of all of Fremont's pictures, just to see who else he might have worked with before.

She was about to do that when the doorbell rang.

"This is a busy place tonight," Sam said from the sofa. He had picked up the Western paperback he was reading from an end table and had been absorbed in it while Phyllis worked on the computer. "You want me to get that?"

"No, I will," Phyllis said. "I don't like to sit there at the desk for too long at one time. I need to get up and move around."

She went into the foyer, wondering who this visitor might be. It was a little late now for someone to be calling.

She opened the door and found Melissa Keller standing there alone, with none of the other movie people accompanying her. As soon as she saw the strained lines of Melissa's face, Phyllis knew something else bad had happened.

"I'm sorry to bother you this late," Melissa began.

"No, that's fine," Phyllis said. "Come in."

As Phyllis closed the door behind her, Melissa said, "You know how you were talking earlier about having a personal stake in those other cases you investigated?"

"That's right, I nearly always did."

"Well, now *I've* got a personal stake. I need to find out who killed Lawrence Fremont, because the police have just arrested my best friend and charged her with murder."

"You mean —"

"That's right," Melissa said. "They claim that it was Julie who killed him."

CHAPTER 16

"Come in," Phyllis said as she overcame her surprise and stepped back.

Melissa came into the foyer and said, "I started to call you, but then I decided it would be better to talk to you in person."

"I'm glad you came over. I want to hear everything you know."

Melissa still wore the same clothes she'd had on for the scenes they were shooting today. Phyllis took her jacket and hung it up, then ushered her into the living room where Sam was already on his feet, having heard the voices in the foyer.

"Miz Keller," he greeted Melissa. "I didn't expect to see you again tonight."

"I didn't expect to be here. And please, Sam, call me Melissa. I think we're all friends here, especially after what happened today. I feel like Phyllis and I are . . . sisters in arms, I guess you'd say. We've both done something that most people haven't."

"Discovered a dead body, you mean," Phyllis said.

"And it's something I'd just as soon never do again!"

"I certainly agree with that. Please, have a seat. Can I get you anything?"

Melissa shook her head as she sat on the same chair where Detective Largo had been earlier. "I had room service sent up when we got back to the hotel. I think just about everybody planned to do that. Nobody felt like going out. Julie asked if she could join me, so we ate together in my room. We were just finishing up when that detective got there."

"Detective Largo?"

"Yes. She had several uniformed officers with her. She asked Julie to step out of the room. I don't think she wanted me involved. But I wasn't going to let Julie face whatever it was alone, so I insisted that she go ahead and say whatever it was she had to say." Melissa shook her head slowly. "I almost wish I hadn't done that, although it wouldn't have changed a thing. The detective said . . ." She had to stop for a couple of seconds before she could go on. "She told Julie that she was under the arrest for the murder of Lawrence Fremont and advised her of her rights."

"How did Julie react to that?"

"How do you *think* she reacted to that?" Melissa asked. "She was shocked and horrified, just like me. Neither of us could believe it. One of the officers handcuffed her — Detective Largo said it was mandatory with an arrest like that — and they led her out, put her in a police car, and took her away. Lord knows what's happening to her now!"

"She'll be all right," Phyllis said, trying to reassure Melissa. "Chief Whitmire's department is very professional. She won't be mistreated, I can promise you that. Have you gotten in touch with a lawyer?"

"Who? All the lawyers I know are in Los Angeles!"

Phyllis nodded. "All right, I can help with that." She looked over at Sam. "Can you call Jimmy?"

"Sure. That's just what I was thinkin'."

As Sam pulled his cell phone from his pocket and left the living room to make the call, Melissa slapped herself lightly on the forehead and said, "Of course. Jimmy D'Angelo. I read about him while I was studying up on your career as a crime-solver. He's the lawyer that you and Sam work for as private eyes, right?"

"Investigators," Phyllis said, "although Sam really does love thinking of himself as a private eye. But yes, Jimmy is a defense attorney, and a very good one. I'm sure he'll do everything he can for Julie and see about getting bail arranged. She probably won't be released until in the morning, though, no matter what Jimmy does."

Melissa slumped back in the chair and shook her head. "Thank you. I just haven't been thinking straight since they took Julie away. We all have rental cars, and as soon as I got my head together, I climbed in mine and came over here. I almost got lost a couple of times, but I found the place. Why in the world would they do such a thing? Have the police in this town lost their minds?"

"I'm sure they think they have a good reason. Detective Largo wouldn't have been able to get an arrest warrant otherwise."

Phyllis thought about telling Melissa that Largo had been over here at the house earlier, but then she decided against it. Largo had gone out on a limb sharing as much information about the case as she had, and Phyllis didn't want to cause trouble for her. Her newfound friendship with Melissa made her want to ease the actress's mind as much as she could, though. She was sort of in the middle here, Phyllis told herself . . . and it wasn't a particularly comfortable position.

Sam came back into the living room, trailed by Carolyn, Eve, and Ronnie. Phyllis supposed they had come downstairs to see who had been at the door. From the worried looks on their faces, Phyllis thought they must have heard what Sam was saying to Jimmy D'Angelo and so had an idea of what was going on.

"Jimmy's on his way to the jail," Sam reported. "He'll let us know what he finds out and whether he's able to do any good for Miz Cordell."

"Thank you, Sam." Phyllis turned back to Melissa. "Do the other members of the movie company know that Julie's been arrested?"

"I doubt it, unless they happened to be around when the cops took her out of the hotel. I think if that were the case, they would have come looking for me. But I don't actually know." Melissa stood up, apparently too nervous to stay sitting down. "Lord, I've got to tell Alan! He'll probably want to call the studio's lawyers."

"I don't know what they can to do help Julie that Jimmy can't," Phyllis said.

Melissa shook her head and said, "Alan's not going to be worried about Julie. He'll want to make sure the studio and the production companies are protected from liability in any lawsuits that come out of this whole mess. They'll leave Julie twisting in the wind as long as their butts are covered!"

"That's just not right," Carolyn said.

"No, it's not, but friendship doesn't mean much when it's stacked up against money." Melissa stood up straighter. "At least it doesn't to most people in this business. But it does to me. I'm not going to turn my back on Julie. Which brings me right back to what I said to you earlier, Phyllis. I *know* that Julie is innocent, and I'll stand a lot better chance of proving that and finding the real killer if you help me, or let me help you, I should say. How about it? Do we solve this case?"

Phyllis had been expecting that question ever since Melissa told her that Julie had been arrested and charged with Lawrence Fremont's murder. She didn't have to think about her answer, either. The insistent prodding of her own desire to learn the truth had already made up her mind.

"We're going to give it our very best effort," she said.

Given the fact that it was fairly late on a Friday evening and Julie's arrest had already taken place, there wasn't really anything that could be done right away, other than getting Jimmy D'Angelo involved in the case. Phyllis persuaded Melissa to go back to the hotel and try to get some rest.

"All right," Melissa said dubiously, "but I don't know how I'm going to sleep after this day. I can't believe how much has happened."

"These things tend to snowball sometimes," Phyllis said.

"There's a saying about bad luck coming in threes. Lawrence's murder, Julie's arrest . . . I can't help but wonder what's going to come next."

"Maybe nothing this time. That *is* just a saying, not a rule."

Melissa managed to smile. "I hope you're right. Still, any time a celebrity dies, the rest of us start looking over our shoulders and don't relax until two more have dropped dead."

After Melissa was gone, Carolyn said, "That's just what we need . . . a murder spree sweeping through that whole bunch of movie people." She looked at Eve. "Although that would give you plenty of fodder for that next book."

"Perish the thought," Eve said. "Next time

I'm going to come up with my own plot, not use something from real life. I was a first-time author with the other book, you know."

Sam said, "And they always tell you to write what you know."

"Let's just all try to get some sleep and see what the situation is in the morning," Phyllis suggested. "I know Melissa doesn't want to accept the idea, but it's possible Julie actually *is* guilty and will have confessed by then."

Carolyn frowned. "Wait a minute. That's like saying *I* might be a murderer, since she's playing me."

"Not at all," Phyllis said quickly before Eve could correct Carolyn about the character of Catherine Whittington not being the same as her.

Carolyn just shook her head and said, "This whole thing is just too much déjà vu for me. But let me know if I can help."

She and Eve went back upstairs, leaving Phyllis, Sam, and Ronnie in the living room. Ronnie asked, "Can I help you investigate, too?"

"I think Phyllis will have all the help she needs," Sam said. "You just worry about school."

"I don't know . . . Maybe if acting doesn't

199

work out, I could become a detective. That Detective Largo seems pretty cool."

"Nothin' wrong with bein' a cop."

"Other than the fact that your mother would be worried about you all the time," Phyllis added.

"You're talking about Mike, aren't you?" Ronnie said. "You really worry about him all the time?"

"Every day," Phyllis said. "But that's what he wanted to do with his life. He's happy, and he's helping people, so I can't really object too much, can I?"

"Your ol' grandpa would worry about you, too," Sam told Ronnie. "But you're a long way from havin' to make up your mind about things like that."

"Not that long," she said. "I'm a senior. Almost grown."

Sam sighed. "Don't remind me."

Ronnie went on upstairs a few minutes later. Sam went back to his book, but he seemed distracted. Phyllis returned to the computer and tried to resume her research into Lawrence Fremont's life and career, but she had trouble concentrating, too. The day's events kept playing out in her mind. Often she felt as if she had seen or heard something that was the key to solving a case, but that impression was missing this time.

She was utterly baffled, and it wasn't a good feeling. She sighed.

"Yeah, me, too," Sam said from the sofa. "Why don't you come over here and sit down? Might be good to just put the whole thing out of your head for a spell. Sometimes your brain works better when you're *not* thinkin' about something."

"You could be right," Phyllis said as she turned off the monitor and stood up. She moved to the sofa, sat down beside him, and leaned her shoulder against his. That felt good. "I don't think my brain *wants* to work anymore, though, especially on some murder. This is *not* how I expected to be spending my retirement years, Sam."

"Nobody expects the Spanish Inquisition."

"What?"

He waved a hand and said, "Just somethin' I saw on TV once. What I mean to say is that life's always gonna have some surprises waitin' for us, some good, some bad, and we just have to do the best we can with 'em. Twenty years ago, if anybody had asked me what I thought was gonna happen between then and now, anything I might've come up with sure wouldn't match how things have really turned out."

"Is that a good thing or a bad thing?"

"It's just a thing," he said with a shrug. "But I'm sure not complainin' about how it's all turned out."

"Neither am I," Phyllis said.

CHAPTER 17

Phyllis wasn't surprised when her phone rang the next morning and the display told her that Jimmy D'Angelo was the caller.

She had just checked the spicy caramel apple pie that was cooling on the counter and found that it was almost ready to go into the container so she could take it to the park for the contest at the festival. She had gotten up early that morning to bake it. In a perfect world, she would have tried out the recipe before now, but this was far from a perfect world. If this pie didn't win or even get an honorable mention, no harm done, of course. These competitions were strictly for fun, as far as she was concerned . . . and another contest of some sort was always right around the corner.

She thumbed the icon on the screen to answer the call and said, "Good morning, Jimmy. I hope you have news."

She didn't specify good new or bad news.

As Sam had said the night before, you had to take what came and make the best of it.

"Good morning," D'Angelo said. "Yeah, I've got news. Ms. Cordell will be out on bail soon. Her release is being processed now. But it wasn't easy. Since the charge is first-degree murder, and since she's from out of town — and Hollywood, at that — the judge really thought she was a flight risk. I talked him out of it, though. That's how good I am."

"Thank you, Jimmy."

"Bail was half a mil, though."

"Good grief," Phyllis said. "That much?"

"His Honor was thinking three-quarters at first. I got a bondsman buddy of mine to go along with the five hundred grand, but I'm not sure he would've taken on the larger amount, so I was glad I haggled the judge down."

"What did Julie tell you? Is she going to plead not guilty?" Phyllis held her breath a little as she waited to hear if Julie had admitted killing Lawrence Fremont. Surely she hadn't, if D'Angelo had gone to the trouble of getting her bail set and arranged.

"She claims up and down that she's innocent, and I believe her. Of course, she's an actor, so it's her job to make people believe what she's saying. That complicates things."

"But your instincts say she didn't do it?"

"My gut does. Same thing. I thought that maybe when they turn her loose, we'd come over there and sit down with you and Sam. You two *are* my top investigators, after all."

"That's fine." Phyllis glanced at the clock on the kitchen wall. "If you can make it in the next hour."

"You have somewhere to be?"

She looked at the pie on the counter and said, "We're going to the Harvest Festival." She felt bad because she was thinking about a pie contest when Julie Cordell's very freedom was at stake, but she had gone to the trouble of baking this one and wanted to enter it.

"Okay," D'Angelo said, sounding a little annoyed. "Anyway, here she comes now, so we'll be there in just a little while."

"Thank you again, Jimmy."

"Hey, what better publicity for a guy like me than defending a Hollywood star against a murder rap?"

He hung up, and Phyllis went to finish getting dressed before D'Angelo and Julie got there. She told Sam that they were on their way, too.

She had just put the pie in the container

when the doorbell rang. Leaving the lid off of it, she went to the foyer and opened the door. Jimmy D'Angelo stood there with Julie beside him. His hand rested lightly on her arm. Her face showed the strain of the night she had just spent in jail.

"Come in," Phyllis said. "Julie, I'm so sorry you're having to go through this."

D'Angelo ushered Julie into the house and on into Phyllis's living room. She sank wearily into one of the comfortable armchairs.

"I'll get you some coffee," Phyllis said, "and there are muffins left from breakfast."

"They gave us breakfast in jail," Julie said in a dull voice.

From the arched entrance between the living room and the foyer, Sam said, "Whatever it was, it wasn't as good as Phyllis's muffins. One of them will make you feel better."

"I can vouch for that," D'Angelo added. He patted his ample stomach.

He was a short, stout man in his forties with a lot of thick, very dark hair. His accent marked him clearly as not a native Texan, but since coming to Weatherford he had established himself as a top defense attorney and a good friend to Phyllis and Sam. They had worked with him on a number of cases.

Julie managed to summon up a faint smile and said, "All right, I'll have one of those muffins. And some good coffee would be wonderful. Thank you."

"Comin' right up," Sam said. He disappeared down the hall toward the kitchen.

"Could I get some, too?" D'Angelo called after him.

"Sure thing!"

Phyllis sat down across from Julie and asked, "Are you all right? They treated you okay?"

"Other than arresting me for murder." A spark of life came back into Julie's eyes. "A murder I didn't commit!"

"We all know that," Phyllis told her.

"Nobody really bothered me, though," Julie went on. "The cops were polite enough, and they put me in a cell by myself, so it's not like they threw me in the drunk tank or something. And Mr. D'Angelo showed up to help me almost before I knew what was going on." She smiled at the attorney, then said to Phyllis, "I really appreciate you asking him to represent me."

"We knew you'd need an attorney," Phyllis said, "and Jimmy's the best."

"How did you even find out about —" Julie stopped short, then said, "Ohhhh. You talked to Melissa, didn't you?"

"She came over here a short time after you were arrested and told us all about it."

"She wants you to find Lawrence's killer and clear my name, doesn't she? And she wants to help you do it."

"Well . . . yes."

"I know her pretty well," Julie went in. "She couldn't really stop talking about that yesterday evening, and seeing me hand-cuffed and marched off that way probably just made her even more determined." She smiled fondly. "I need to let her know that I'm all right. I'm sure she's worried."

"I'm sure she is, too," Phyllis agreed. "Right now, though —"

"Right now, folks need to try these muffins," Sam said as he walked into the room carrying a plate with several of them on it. Carolyn came along behind him with cups of coffee for Julie and D'Angelo. She had been in the kitchen when Sam got there.

For a few minutes, silence mostly reigned in the living room as the visitors sampled the muffins. Sam, who was nearly a bottomless pit where food was concerned, helped himself to one as well, although he'd already had two at breakfast, Phyllis recalled. D'Angelo washed down the last bite of his muffin with a sip of coffee, then said, "We need to talk about the case."

Phyllis, who was keeping an eye on the time, nodded and said, "Yes, we do."

Before they could begin, however, the doorbell rang again. Carolyn went to answer it and came back with Melissa Keller.

"Julie!" Melissa said. Julie stood up and the two of them embraced. Melissa stepped back and went on, "I came to talk to Phyllis, but I had a feeling you might be here, too." She turned to D'Angelo and held out her hand. "I'm Melissa Keller."

"Jimmy D'Angelo," he introduced himself. "It's an honor to meet you, Ms. Keller. I enjoy your work."

"I hope we all enjoy yours," Melissa said as she shook hands with him. "That'll mean you've gotten rid of this crazy murder charge against Julie."

"We were just about to discuss that . . ."

"Goodness, don't let me stop you." Melissa's eyes fell on the plate of muffins sitting on the coffee table. "Did you make those, Phyllis?"

"Actually, no. They're Carolyn's."

"I know you're a wonderful baker, too, Carolyn, so I'm going to help myself. The rest of you go ahead with what you were doing."

D'Angelo stayed on his feet and faced all

of them as he said, "I hope you'll forgive me, Ms. Cordell, but I'm going to fill Phyllis and Sam in on what I've learned, and I'll have to be kind of blunt about some things."

Julie nodded. "I understand. There's nothing quite as blunt as being arrested."

"I talked to Isabel Largo and to the assistant district attorney who got the arrest warrant. The warrant was issued largely on the basis of motive, since all the physical evidence is still being examined. Largo and the ADA were both cagey about it, but my hunch is that they don't have any eyewitness testimony to tie you to the killing, Ms. Cordell. The cops were feeling some pressure to make an arrest, though, and they settled on you instead of your niece, although I'm not quite sure why."

"Your niece?" Phyllis repeated.

Julie sighed and nodded. "Becca Peterson. She's my sister's daughter."

"I didn't know that," Melissa said in a surprised tone.

"Neither did I," Phyllis said.

"Not that many people do," Julie said. "Becca has a very independent streak. She didn't want anybody thinking that she got cast in roles because of my influence. Although Lord knows why she would think that. I don't really *have* any influence. No aging character actress does."

"You're more than that," Melissa protested.

Julie shook her head and said, "Not really."

Melissa frowned, leaned forward, and asked, "Then the rumors about Lawrence and Becca are true?"

"They are. He pressured her into having an affair with him. Becca wanted to break it off, but Lawrence wouldn't allow that. It would have been too big a blow to his pride. He had to be the one to decide when it was over. She told him she would go public with her accusations, and he said he'd ruin her in Hollywood if she did."

"In this day and age?" Carolyn said. "I don't think he'd have the power to do that. In fact, I'd say it's the other way around. Much bigger men than Lawrence Fremont have been taken down by accusations like that."

Julie nodded and said, "That's true. But Becca backed off anyway. She didn't want to take the chance, just as she was getting her career established."

"So the cops decided that you took care of the problem for her," D'Angelo said.

Julie shook her head and said, "I wouldn't have done that. I may have hated Lawrence Fremont, but I wouldn't have killed him."

"Of course you didn't, honey!" Melissa said. "The whole idea is crazy."

"I don't believe they can prove that you did," D'Angelo said. "It's best that we never even go to trial and risk it, though." He looked at Phyllis and Sam. "That means finding out who really killed the guy."

Phyllis said, "I know you'd probably like to go back to the hotel, Julie, so you can get some actual rest . . ."

"I need a shower first," Julie said. "I know it wasn't really that bad, but just being in jail . . ." She shuddered. "It makes a person feel dirty."

"It certainly does," Carolyn agreed fervently. "I know."

"The police have established that Lawrence Fremont was poisoned by cyanide, and that it was probably put into a piece of the pecan pie I took to the park yesterday," Phyllis went on. "The killer must have put that pie right into his hand and watched him eat it, just to make sure it didn't wind up being eaten by some innocent person."

"And to watch him die," Melissa added. "Whoever it was must have taken some satisfaction in that, otherwise they wouldn't have chosen such a method."

The same thought had occurred to Phyllis the night before. She nodded and said, "I think Fremont must have been in the motor home he was using when that happened. It was parked across the street, so the killer must have gotten the pie from the craft services table, walked across the park and the street to the motor home, and knocked on the door. Fremont let the killer in and took the pecan pie and ate it."

"Maybe the killer claimed the pie was a peace offerin'," Sam suggested. "That'd mean that he — or she — had had trouble with him in the past."

"Lord, who *didn't* Lawrence have trouble with?" Melissa said. "A couple of years ago, he and Bob Harkness punched each other out on the set one day. I wasn't there because I wasn't in that picture, but from what I heard, it was quite a brawl."

D'Angelo asked, "Who's this Harkness? The name's familiar, but I can't place him."

Sam looked around, maybe to make sure Eve wasn't in the vicinity to correct him, Phyllis thought, then said, "He plays me in the movie. Seems like a pretty good guy."

Melissa blew out a breath of air at that comment.

Phyllis seized the opportunity to ask, "Why is it that the two of you don't get along, Melissa?"

"Picked up on that, did you? Of course

you did. You're the detective. Look, I'm not saying that Bob Harkness is a bad guy, and I'm certainly not saying that he's a killer, but he's the most arrogant son of a . . . gun . . . I've ever run into, and that's saying a lot because I've worked in Hollywood for the past thirty years! I did a guest shot on that series he did for one of the streaming platforms, and he starts trying to give *me* lessons on how to improve my performance. They kept having to reshoot scenes because he couldn't even talk like an American instead of a dang Aussie half the time, and he's lecturing *me* on acting! Well, I told him what he could do with his advice." Melissa paused and smiled ruefully. "And now I'm getting carried away, aren't I? It's just that when you've been around as long as I have, it really rubs you the wrong way when somebody with a fraction of the experience starts telling you how to do things."

Jimmy D'Angelo said, "The important thing here is that this Harkness has an old grudge against the victim. He had a reason for wanting Fremont dead, too."

"What about Earl Thorpe?" Phyllis said.

Melissa and Julie both looked at her. "Earl?" Julie said. "He's the sweetest guy in the world."

"He really is," Melissa agreed.

"But he's the assistant director, and he's been doing a lot of work on the picture that Fremont should have been doing. Fremont would have taken the credit for it, too."

"You bet he would have," Melissa said.

"But now Thorpe has taken over the picture," Phyllis continued. "That's bound to reflect well on him . . ."

She stopped as she saw Melissa shaking her head.

"Alan said this morning that he's already talking to Clive Walker about finishing the rest of the picture once we get back to Austin."

"Who's Walker?" D'Angelo asked.

"Another A-list director. Well, high B-list, anyway. Alan trusts Earl to shoot the rest of the footage we need to get here, but he's not going to turn the whole thing over to him."

Phyllis said, "Would Thorpe have known that, though?"

"Well . . . he could have hoped that Alan would give the job to him, I suppose."

"That's another motive. Fremont has been making life miserable for those screenwriters, too. There's no real shortage of suspects." Phyllis turned to Julie again. "What about an alibi? Where were you during lunch yesterday? That must have been when the killer took the pie to Fremont."

"I was with the rest of the cast most of the time," Julie said.

"But not *all* the time?" D'Angelo asked.

"Not every minute," Julie snapped. "I went to the restroom, and I walked around the park some. You stand and wait so much when you're shooting a picture, so I like to move around when I get the chance."

"I feel the same way," Carolyn told her.

Phyllis nodded slowly and said, "With so many people in the park, and so much going on, it's going to be very difficult for the police to find anyone who can state definitively that they saw anyone doing anything."

"Especially at a particular time," D'Angelo added. "We can cast reasonable doubt on any such testimony. Still, it's mighty hard to prove a negative in the minds of a jury."

Julie put her hands on her knees, sighed, and said, "Can we postpone the rest of this discussion? Honestly, I'm exhausted, and I just can't think straight right now."

"Of course you can't," Melissa said. "I'll take you back to the hotel and get you settled in."

"And we need to get to the park," Phyllis said. "The festival should be getting underway already."

"You're going to attend?" Melissa asked.

"Yes, I decided to go ahead and enter a pie in the contest. Just *not* a pecan pie."

"I'll see you there, then, once I'm sure Julie's all right."

"You're coming to the festival?"

"There's no location shooting today," Melissa said, "and I think it'd be a good idea if we took another look at the crime scene, don't you, partner?"

CHAPTER 18

Sam drove his pickup again and took Ronnie with him, while Carolyn and Eve went with Phyllis in the Lincoln. The big car had enough room for all five of them, but it would have been more crowded.

"I can't believe I missed everything exciting this morning!" Ronnie had said before they left the house. "You shouldn't have let me sleep in."

"We have enough trouble gettin' you up for school," Sam had told her. "Figured there wasn't any point in fightin' that battle on a Saturday, as long as you were up in time to go to the festival."

"I suppose I can't argue with that. And you didn't solve the case yet, right?" she asked Phyllis.

"Far from it."

"Good. I wouldn't want to miss that." Ronnie snagged one of the remaining muffins as she went through the kitchen to leave with Sam.

Now, as she drove toward the park, Phyllis said, "Ronnie thinks it's just a given that I'm going to figure out who the killer is."

"Of course she does," Carolyn said from the passenger seat. "You always do."

"One of these days there's going to be a case that's too tough for me to solve."

In the back seat, Eve said, "I doubt that. Since I missed the discussion, too, why don't you tell me about it on the way over there? That might help you get your thoughts in order."

It couldn't hurt, Phyllis knew, so as she battled the traffic on South Main to get to the park, she went through as much as she could remember about what had been said earlier in the living room.

"I just don't believe Jason or Deanne could be guilty of such a thing," Eve said when Phyllis was finished.

"Why?" Carolyn asked. "Because they're writers?"

"We tend to live vicariously."

Carolyn turned in the seat to look at her and said, "Ha! You've never experienced anything vicariously in your life, Eve Turner. You've always had to get right in there and go for it yourself."

"I suppose that's true, but I think most

writers, if they had a grudge against somebody, they'd just kill them off in a book or something. Or at least base an unflattering character on them."

Carolyn cocked an eyebrow. "Is that what you do?"

Eve ignored that question and asked Phyllis, "Why would Jason or Deanne have a reason to want Lawrence Fremont dead?"

"You saw the way he lit into them about the script yesterday," Phyllis said. "He's been doing that all along, hasn't he?"

"I suppose so, but would they kill him just because he criticized their work? If that was true, a lot of critics would be dead! Anyway, it was mostly Jason he was unhappy with, and Jason's no murderer. You might as well accuse a . . . a sad little puppy!"

"He is pretty pathetic," Carolyn said. "It wouldn't surprise me if his wife is cheating on him."

Phyllis said, "Teddy Demming was trying to comfort him yesterday."

"Who?" Carolyn asked.

"That production assistant with the long dark hair and the Brooklyn accent."

"Oh, her," Carolyn said. "I remember seeing her."

"You saw her with Jason, Phyllis?" Eve asked.

"Just briefly. She seemed to be trying to cheer him up. It must not have worked, though, since he went off and got drunk." Phyllis made the turn onto the road leading to the park. "And even if there is something going on between them, I can't see any way that connects with Fremont's murder."

"What about Fremont and Deanne Wilkes?" Carolyn asked Eve. "Could there be something between them?"

"I've never heard anything about it if there is," Eve said. "It's possible, though."

"It's Hollywood," Carolyn said in a disgusted tone. "Until I see proof otherwise, I'm just going to assume that they're *all* sleeping with each other."

Phyllis surveyed the parking situation ahead of her, which was considerably different today. The delay in getting here while she had talked with Julie, Melissa, and D'Angelo had given the festival time to get crowded.

"I think we're going to have to walk some," she told her friends. Cars were already parked along both sides of the road.

"I was afraid of that, so I wore good shoes for it," Carolyn said.

Phyllis found an empty spot and carefully maneuvered the Lincoln into it. One of these days she was going to have to get a new car, she told herself, one with all those new-fangled accessories like a back-up camera and parking assist . . . although she wasn't sure she completely trusted such technology.

They got out and started walking toward the park, with Eve carrying the spicy caramel apple pie. "Don't let it out of your sight," Carolyn warned her. "The killer could try to strike again. Maybe it was a lunatic who murdered Mr. Fremont. He could come back and try to take out the whole park today."

"I wouldn't talk too much about that," Phyllis cautioned. "You might cause a panic."

"A good panic comes in handy sometimes," Carolyn said.

With Carolyn being one of the festival's organizers, they didn't have to join the line of people with bags of canned food waiting to get in. Earlier in the week, Phyllis, Sam, and Carolyn had loaded the back of Sam's pickup with cases of canned food and taken it to the food pantry, so they had more than done their part. Carolyn led them to a checkpoint where volunteers were admitted. Orange plastic fence had been stretched around the part to control the crowds, but there were several entrance points. Sam and

Ronnie knew to come to this one when they arrived. They might, in fact, already be here.

Tables were set up in front of the caretaker's cottage for the entries in the pie contest. Phyllis added hers to the array of delicious-looking pies and filled out an entry form. The woman supervising everything wished her good luck and added, "The judging will be at two o'clock."

"We'll be here," Phyllis promised.

As they walked away, Eve asked, "How many judges do they have?"

"Three," Carolyn replied. "A member of the city council, the director of the Chamber of Commerce, and somebody from the Lion's Club, I'm not sure who."

"There's going to be a lot of leftover pie, isn't there? I mean, with all those different ones to taste, they can't eat big slices. My goodness, I'd get so full I'd burst!"

"After the contest, the pies will be sold, with the proceeds going to the food pantry," Carolyn explained. "You knew that, didn't you, Phyllis?"

"Of course. I knew they'd be going to a fundraiser. The more money for the pantry, the better."

"There are Sam and Ronnie," Eve said.

The two of them were coming from the direction of the parking lot. Ronnie said something to Sam, then veered off along one of the other concrete paths. Phyllis knew the girl wanted to go around the festival and look for some of her friends.

Sam joined them, grinned, and said, "Sort of a madhouse here today, isn't it?"

"There's already a really good crowd," Phyllis said, "and it'll just get busier as the day goes on, I imagine."

The food vendors all had customers lined up. Potential buyers browsed through the arts and crafts displays where most of the items were also for sale. Children thronged the playground area. People were everywhere Phyllis looked, all the way down to the lake's edge. The picnic areas on the far side of the water were packed as well. The smells of charcoal and roasting meat drifted across the lake. The noise level was high but not overpowering. Everyone seemed to be having a good time. No doubt some members of the crowd had come to the park today because they knew a murder had taken place there the day before, but it wasn't casting a pall over the celebration, at least so far.

However, a considerable crowd was gathered around the log cabin with the dogtrot where Lawrence Fremont's body had been found. Phyllis couldn't see into the dogtrot from where they were. She said, "They didn't go ahead and put the scarecrow in there, did they?"

"I don't know," Sam said. "We can go take a look. That's probably where Miz Keller will head once she gets here. She said she wanted the two of you to study it."

"I know what she said. I'm just not sure I feel like doing that." Phyllis sighed. "On the other hand, I promised we'd try to help Julie, so I guess I can't really avoid it forever."

"We're coming with you," Carolyn declared.

"I appreciate that. The more friends around, the better."

The four of them had to walk toward the lake to reach one of the paths that would take them in the right direction. They could have cut across the park, but at their age it was better to walk on a nice flat surface. As they neared the cabin, Phyllis tried to peer through gaps in the crowd, but they were almost there before she could see that not only was there no scarecrow, but the hay bales had been removed as well. The dogtrot was empty now, except for people who were walking through it or standing around talking.

"Not much to see here," Carolyn commented. "I can't say I'm disappointed by that, either."

Phyllis looked through the dogtrot and up the slight hill toward the road. The motor homes used by the movie company weren't parked up there today, and neither were the equipment trucks or the SUVs. All of them would have been in sight from this point the day before, although anyone looking in that direction might not have been able to see the motor homes except for their upper parts, because of the slope.

"We've talked about who had a reason to want Lawrence Fremont dead," she mused, "but we haven't talked about the way he was dressed up in that scarecrow outfit, or how the body got down here. I wonder what sort of theory the police have about *that*."

"One thing seems pretty obvious to me," Sam said. "Fremont wasn't a big fella, but Miz Cordell couldn't have picked up his body and hauled it all the way from that motor home on the other side of the road. It'd take a good-sized man to do that."

"Like Alan Sammons or Earl Thorpe," Phyllis said.

Carolyn asked, "What about Jason Wilkes?"

"When it comes to bein' physically fit, he seemed one step above puddin' to me," Sam said. "I think his wife would come closer to bein' able to do that."

"What's the significance of him being dressed as a scarecrow to start with?" Phyllis asked. "Was the killer trying to send a message? That doesn't fit with Julie, either."

Carolyn said, "They're just flailing around and they happened to land on her. The district attorney probably ordered Chief Whitmire to make an arrest whether they had any evidence or not."

"That doesn't sound like the sort of thing the chief would do."

"You know what a publicity hog the DA is. Putting a movie star on trial for murder would get him a lot of press. Maybe he's planning on running for Congress, or even state attorney general."

That was entirely possible, given the ambition that the man had displayed in the past, Phyllis thought, but she still didn't believe the police would have arrested Julie Cordell unless there was some legitimate reason to believe she was guilty. The hidden relationship with Becca Peterson wasn't the strongest motive Phyllis had ever come across . . . but it wasn't the weakest, either.

"There you are," a voice said. They turned to see that Melissa Keller had come up to them. "I figured I'd find you here, Phyllis. Have you come up with anything?"

"Not yet. But we haven't been here long."

Melissa looked into the empty dogtrot and said, "Man, they cleaned it out, didn't they? What do you think happened to everything?"

"The bales Mr. Fremont's body was sitting on would have been impounded as evidence. The others are probably being used as decorations in places around the park."

"I guess whoever was in charge of decorations figured it would be in bad taste to put out the prop scarecrow."

Carolyn said, "That's the decision I would have made if it had been up to me."

Melissa stiffened abruptly and said in an angry voice, "It's that cop."

Phyllis turned to look where Melissa was looking and saw that she was right.

Detective Isabel Largo was making her way through the crowd toward the log cabin, and from the intent expression on her face, she wasn't just visiting the festival. She was looking for something . . . or some-one.

CHAPTER 19

It quickly became obvious who Isabel Largo was looking for. She walked up to the group beside the cabin, crossed her arms, and glared at Phyllis.

"I thought we weren't going to be at cross-purposes on this case, Mrs. Newsom," she said. "But who should show up almost before Ms. Cordell was booked other than Jimmy D'Angelo."

"Julie has a right to an attorney," Phyllis said. "She doesn't know any here in Weatherford."

"So you don't deny that you got D'Angelo involved?"

"Why would I deny that?"

"If I'd known we were going to wind up on opposite sides, I wouldn't have given you as much information as I did. I wouldn't have shared anything with you."

Melissa said, "Wait a minute. *You* consulted Phyllis, too?"

Largo ignored that and went on to Phyllis, "The smartest thing for you to do is stay out of this. There's going to be a lot of publicity, and it won't reflect well on you that you're trying to get an outsider off on a murder charge, especially an outsider from Hollywood."

Sam said, "Why would folks in Weatherford care about that? The victim was from Hollywood, too. No offense, Detective, but I've got a hunch the whole town's stockin' up on popcorn right about now, figurin' it's gonna be quite a show."

"You don't have any real evidence against Julie Cordell," Phyllis said. "You have a possible motive, and a rather flimsy one at that. Nothing else."

"That's not exactly true. We know the poison that killed Lawrence Fremont was delivered in a piece of pecan pie that you brought to the park. The pie was found in Fremont's stomach. A piece of crust was found in the motor home he was using, so that places the murder weapon on the scene with him."

That bit about the piece of crust was new information. Phyllis didn't know whether Largo had let it slip intentionally, or was just carried away by her irritation. The detective wasn't finished, though.

"We also found traces of pecan pie in the pocket of Julie Cordell's jeans," Largo went on. "That's proof she had the murder weapon in her possession."

Melissa said, "Now hold on just a minute. There's no way in the world somebody could stick a slice of pie in a pants pocket like that! There wouldn't be room for it."

"She got the pie on her hand when she took it to Fremont's motor home, and then later she stuck her hand in her pocket, after she'd poisoned him. That's how the traces of it got in there." Largo's voice was cold and hostile as she replied.

"Were there also traces of cyanide in Julie's pocket?" Phyllis asked.

Largo just glared some more and didn't answer.

"That's what I thought," Phyllis said. "So all the evidence really proves is that Julie handled a slice of pie sometime during the day. You can't be sure it was the same slice that had the poison in it."

"The lab's still working on that," Largo snapped.

"If the lab finds cyanide, you might have a case. You'd still need testimony from someone who saw Julie take the pie into the motor home."

"Maybe we do," Largo said evasively.

Phyllis didn't believe that. She said, "What's your theory about the scarecrow? Why dress Fremont's body that way? How do you think Julie got the body from a motor home all the way up there" — she pointed toward the road — "to the dogtrot down here? She's not big enough to have carried a corpse that far, even though Fremont wasn't a large man."

Before Largo could answer — not that Phyllis believed Largo even *had* a good answer for any of those questions — Melissa said, "You should be talking to Earl Thorpe."

Phyllis and Largo both frowned at her. "Thorpe?" Largo repeated. "The assistant director?"

"That's right." Melissa sighed. "I got to thinking about what we talked about earlier, Phyllis, how Earl might have figured he was going to take over the picture permanently. After I got Julie back to her hotel room, I went down to the lobby to come over here. Before I walked out, though, I saw Earl and Alan talking in the parking lot. Earl looked upset, and I swear, I thought he was going to take a swing at Alan. They argued for a few minutes, and then Earl stomped off somewhere. I went out and asked Alan what was wrong, and he said Earl was mad because Clive Walker agreed to take over the picture. So you were right. Earl had his sights set on it."

"That doesn't mean he killed Fremont," Largo said. "All that could have happened whether he had anything to do with Fremont's death or not."

Melissa shrugged. "Maybe. But if you want to avoid looking like a fool, Detective, you might want to start thinking about digging deeper, instead of being so sure you've got it all figured out."

Largo bit back whatever response she was about to make, then turned on her heel and stalked away.

"Well, she's a mite unhappy," Sam drawled.

"She probably knows her case against Julie is weak," Phyllis said, "but she's going to defend it anyway. I have to admit, the business about them finding traces of pie in Julie's clothes is troubling."

Melissa said, "All that proves is that she ate a piece of pie!"

"Did you see her do that?"

"Well . . . no." Melissa frowned. "I'm trying to think back. You know the pie container had a hands-off note on it."

Phyllis nodded. "I assume someone took that off and opened the container when it was time for lunch."

"Yeah, by the time I went through the line and got my food, it was half gone."

"Did you get a piece of it?" Phyllis asked.

Melissa shook her head. "No, like I told you a couple of nights ago, I try to avoid sweets as much as I can." Her eyes widened slightly. "I know who *did* have a slice, though. Deanne Wilkes. I saw her eating it."

"What about her husband?"

"He was nowhere around, as far as I remember."

That was during the time Jason had been holed up somewhere drinking, Phyllis recalled. But he could have ventured out long enough to get something to eat.

"I walked by there again a little later and the pie was all gone," Melissa continued. "I remember not being surprised that it was popular, but that's all. At that point, nobody knew it was going to be important, so I didn't really pay that much attention."

"I don't imagine anyone did," Phyllis said.

"Except the killer," Sam said. "Whoever did it was countin' on the crowd and the confusion makin' it hard for anybody to recall anything for sure." He waved a hand at everything going on around them. "It wasn't this bad yesterday, but almost."

"The police won't actually question everyone who was here yesterday," Melissa said. "That would be too big a job, and anyway, they believe they've already arrested the killer." She looked at Phyllis. "That's why it's up to you and me . . . and we're not going to let Julie down."

Phyllis sympathized with Melissa's determination to clear her friend's name. She had felt the same way when *her* friends had come under suspicion of murder.

However, right now there wasn't much she could do, so she felt like they might as well try to enjoy the festival. For the next couple of hours they strolled around the park, checking out all the arts and crafts and snacking on food from the various vendors. From time to time they sat down at one of the tables to rest for a few minutes.

Somewhat to Phyllis's surprise, Melissa went along with them. She talked about some of the previous cases in which Phyllis had been involved and questioned her about her methods of solving them.

"I've still got a movie to finish, you know," she pointed out. "I want my performance to be as true to life as I can make it."

During one of those breaks, Deanne Wilkes walked up to the table and asked, "Is it all right if I join you ladies . . . and you, too, of course, Mr. Fletcher?"

"Of course," Eve said. "I didn't really expect to see you here today."

"It's something to do. No offense, but this isn't exactly the most exciting town I've ever been in."

"Where's Jason this morning?"

Deanne shrugged and shook her head. "I don't have any idea. He was gone when I woke up. He may have flown back to L.A. for all I know — or care."

"He'll be in trouble with the police if he did," Phyllis said. "None of you were supposed to leave town."

Deanne frowned and said, "Really? Is that still a thing? I thought since Julie was arrested, it was all over."

"She didn't do it," Melissa snapped. "She's innocent."

"The investigation hasn't been closed officially, as far as I know," Phyllis said.

"Well, I'm not leaving town until everybody else does, obviously," Deanne said. "The script might still need some rewrites, and since Jason's not around, that leaves it up to me, doesn't it?"

Carolyn asked, "Are they still going to do that scene with the scarecrow the way it was written? I think that would be terrible now."

Melissa sighed and nodded. "I haven't

talked to Alan or Earl about it yet, but I don't see any way of getting out of it. I mean, Peggy Nelson still has to discover that body one way or another, doesn't she? Even if Deanne tweaks the script a little, the whole movie is about the murder, so it has to take place."

"Maybe I could have somebody else find the victim, though," Deanne said, "if it's going to be too hard for you to play that scene."

Melissa shook her head determinedly. "No. I'm a professional. Good Lord, if I can stand to kiss Bob Harkness, I can do this!"

"Bob's not that bad," Deanne said.

"Yeah, well, you haven't ever . . . Wait a minute." Melissa leaned forward and looked intently at the blond screenwriter. "Deanne, you and Harkness, you've never . . . Good Lord, you're blushing! You have!"

"It's none of your business what I've done," Deanne snapped as she abruptly got to her feet.

"Poor Jason," Eve said.

"Poor Jason?" Deanne repeated with an incredulous look. "You've met the guy. Any problems Jason has, I promise you he's brought them on himself. If that little Teddy bitch can't see that, it's her look-out." She turned and stalked away.

Phyllis watched her go and mused, "So there *is* something going on between Jason and Teddy."

"Maybe," Melissa said. "I hadn't heard anything about Deanne and Harkness, though, or seen any signs of it. I'm not really surprised, though, after what happened between her and Lawrence."

All the other eyes around the table swung to stare at her.

"Deanne and Fremont?" Phyllis said after a moment.

"Yeah. It was a while ago. Those were the rumors, anyway, and I don't know of any reason *not* to believe them." Melissa placed her hands on the edge of the concrete table. "Listen, Lawrence Fremont liked women, liked them a lot, and he went after anybody who struck his fancy, as they used to say. I've heard stories about him going all the way back to New York, in his theater days."

Phyllis nodded. "There was a young actress who committed suicide, and it was suspected that her involvement with Fremont may have contributed to that."

"You *have* done your research."

Carolyn said, "Are you sure the poor young woman's death really was suicide? Could it have been murder? Could Fremont have been involved? If he was, that might be connected somehow to his murder."

"I didn't find even a hint of that in anything I read," Phyllis said.

"I don't really believe it, either," Melissa added. "Lawrence was a horndog, no doubt about it, and he might lose his temper and throw a punch at another guy, but I never heard anything about him abusing women except with the power he wielded."

Carolyn sniffed and said, "That's bad enough."

"Yes, it is. He could be very . . . insistent."

Phyllis looked at her and raised an eyebrow. "You sound like you're speaking from experience."

"No, I just . . ." Melissa sighed. "Okay, you've got me. But it was twenty-five years ago. One of the first features where I had more than a walk-on part. Lawrence was still a rising star when it came to directing, but he *was* a star. I figured it couldn't hurt my career, you know?"

"That's terrible," Eve murmured.

"You mean terrible that he pressured me into it?" Melissa laughed. "I wasn't a kid. I knew what it meant to make it to the big leagues. In those days, you went along to get along, you know what I mean? Nobody regarded it as any big deal."

"It *was* a big deal," Eve said, "but actually I was talking about the way you found the body of someone you'd been close to, even if what happened was years ago."

"Honey, I'm not sure it made any difference. That was so long ago it seems like prehistoric times now. I've worked with Lawrence on three or four other pictures. It never came up again. We'd both long since moved on."

Phyllis thought for a second and then asked, "What about Julie?"

"What about her?"

"Was she ever involved with Fremont?"

Without hesitation, Melissa shook her head and said, "Absolutely not. She's not his type and never has been. Anyway, I think this is the first picture she's been in that he directed. He never would have had the opportunity to try to pressure her into anything."

Phyllis made a mental note to look up that assertion and see if it was true. With the Internet, it would be easy enough to check out all the movies in which Julie had appeared.

"Is there anyone else working on this picture he might have gone after in the past?"

"Not that I can think of," Melissa said.

"Of course, I didn't know that anything had ever gone on between him and Deanne, so maybe I'm not as well-informed as I thought I was."

"You said you saw Deanne eating some of the pie . . . Maybe she thought —"

Melissa slapped a hand down on the table and said excitedly, "Maybe she thought that when she and Jason were hired to write the script for this movie, she could start something with Lawrence again. But then she found out that he was already mixed up with Becca! That could have made her mad enough to want to get back at Lawrence. That's motive, and we know she had some of the pie, so that's means, and with everything that was going on yesterday, nobody's ever going to be able to pin down opportunity." She sat back in satisfaction. "That's every bit as good a case as the cops have against Julie. Better, even. Is Detective Largo still around? We need to talk to her."

Eve said, "I really don't think Deanne would do such a thing."

"You like her because she's a writer," Melissa snapped. "Well, *I* don't think Julie would kill anybody."

Phyllis said, "We don't have any actual evidence against Deanne. It's all just speculation."

241

"That was enough for them to arrest Julie."

"Yes, but we won't get them to back off on that by giving them an option that's not really any stronger."

"What about that argument I saw Earl having with Alan?"

"It's the same thing," Phyllis said. "A plausible theory, but nothing more."

Melissa sighed and slowly nodded. "I guess you're right. I got carried away there for a minute, but the only thing that's going to save Julie is evidence, and we don't have any. But we're going to keep looking, aren't we?"

"Yes," Phyllis said, "we are." She checked the time on her phone. "Right now, though, the judging for the pie contest is coming up soon."

CHAPTER 20

They hadn't eaten any actual lunch, but during the morning and the first part of the afternoon they had snacked enough on pretzels, sausage-on-a-stick, chili, caramel corn, and cotton candy that no one needed a full meal. Phyllis felt rather like she'd had one as they walked toward the area of the park where the pie contest was being held.

Melissa came along, although she was obviously still distracted by the theories they had come up with regarding Lawrence Fremont's murder.

Those scenarios were still percolating in the back of Phyllis's brain, too. This was as complex a case as she had encountered: a victim with plenty of enemies and therefore plenty of suspects; a murder that had taken place in the midst of a crowd that created confusion and obscured the facts; a bizarre angle that made no sense at all in the way the corpse had been dressed as a scarecrow and propped up for someone to find.

The sight of all the pies spread out on the tables distracted Phyllis from those bewildering thoughts. She told herself sternly that for a few minutes, she was going to forget about murder and concentrate on something more pleasant.

And this array of delicious-looking pies was definitely pleasant. There were all kinds: apple, peach, cherry, lemon, key lime, pecan, pumpkin, sweet potato, strawberry, rhubarb, cream pies, custard pies, cobblers, tarts, meringues, pies with cross-hatched top crusts, pies with solid top crusts, chocolate, coconut, buttermilk pies . . .

Sam was equally impressed. "Dang," he said in an awed voice, "that's a veritable plethora of pies."

"I know what the words mean," Eve said, "but I've never heard them applied to pies."

"It's somethin' Howard Cosell used to say, just not about pies. Got to admit, the description fits."

A good-sized crowd had gathered in front of the tables. The judges, two women and one man, were ready to begin sampling the entries. One of the women took on the job of cutting a small slice from each pie, then dividing it into three even smaller slices. Even doing that, the judges might be a little sick of pie by the time they finished with this task, Phyllis thought.

A lot of talk and laughter went on among the spectators as the judging continued, but the judges themselves seemed to take their job seriously. Phyllis mentioned that to Carolyn, who nodded and said, "As well they should. It's quite an honor to have your pie picked as the best of the Harvest Festival."

Melissa said, "These contests are important to you, aren't they, Phyllis?"

"Well, they're hardly important in the big scheme of things, of course," Phyllis said. "But I admit, I have a competitive nature, in this one area, anyway."

"Sometimes there are prizes," Carolyn added. "Mostly, though, it's just the recognition of your hard work and creativity that counts. That makes you feel like you haven't been wasting your time. Any artist likes that feeling."

Eve said, "You aren't comparing baking a pie to writing a novel or painting a picture, are you?"

"Or making a movie?" Melissa said.

"In every one of those things, you put various ingredients together in a certain way unique to yourself, and when you're done, you have something that never existed before," Carolyn insisted. "I don't see any difference."

She had a point there, Phyllis thought, and Eve and Melissa seemed to see it, too. Eve said, "Well, if you're going to put it like that . . ."

Sam nudged Phyllis and said, "They're fixin' to taste your pie. Y'all can discuss creative philosophy later."

The judge with the knife cut a slice of Phyllis's pie and then divided it for the others. Phyllis watched their expressions closely as they ate the samples. She could tell they were all trying to maintain poker faces, but she was convinced that she saw pleasure in their eyes. The odds were high today, but she told herself that she had a shot in this contest.

The judges moved on and continued tasting the remaining entries for another ten or fifteen minutes. Then they withdrew to the front porch of the caretaker's cottage to confer about their decision. When they returned to the tables after several long minutes, one of the female judges picked up several of the pies and moved them to a cleared area on the table at the end of the line. Phyllis caught her breath as she saw the judge include the pie she had brought to the park today.

When six finalists had been selected, the judges converged on that half-dozen and sampled them again.

"The winner and five runners-up, I reckon," Sam said as they watched.

"Yes, that's right," Phyllis said.

"And your pie is one of 'em."

Melissa squeezed Phyllis's arm and said, "Good luck. Not that you need it."

"Everybody can always use a little good luck," Phyllis said, not taking her eyes off the judges now.

The three of them put their heads together for another low-voiced conversation, then one of the women picked up a pie and announced loudly, "The lemon chess is the winner!"

"Oh, no," Melissa moaned. "You didn't win."

"But she was one of the runners-up," Sam said. "That's not bad in a contest with this many pies in it."

"No, it's not," Phyllis said. She had felt a tiny twinge of disappointment when the judge picked up someone else's pie, but it lasted for only a second before a sense of satisfaction replaced it. She knew she had done good work. So had the person who'd baked the lemon chess pie. It was all good.

"All the pies are now for sale," the male

judge announced. "Ten dollars each, with the proceeds going to the food pantry!"

The crowd surged forward as people began claiming the various pies.

"I'll try to buy yours," Sam told Phyllis.

"No, you should get one of the others," she said. "You eat my cooking all the time."

"You haven't heard any complaints from me, have you?"

"Just get something that looks good to you."

He ventured into the melee and came back grinning with a cherry pie in his hands. "Always had a soft spot for a good cherry pie," he said.

It looked good, all right. Phyllis could tell just by looking at it that the golden-brown crust would be light and flaky, and the delicately crimped rim around the outside wasn't browned too much, which was always a tricky balance to strike. It had taken her a long time as a young baker to get down the knack of making a crust so that the pie could bake long enough without burning the edge of the crust.

"Let's go sit down and sample that bad boy," Melissa suggested.

They all got plastic forks and small paper plates from stacks on one of the portable tables, then found a place at a concrete picnic table to sit down. Sam had a plastic knife to cut the pie, but before he could do so, Ronnie walked up and said, "I hope there's enough of that so I can have a piece, too."

"Sure, I reckon we can divide it up so there's enough to go around. Where have you been?"

"Here in the park," Ronnie replied, gesturing vaguely. "A lot of my friends are here." She looked at Phyllis. "You haven't solved the murder yet, have you? I don't want to miss out on that."

"No, I'm not even thinking about it right now," Phyllis said.

Melissa nudged her with an elbow and said, "Maybe you should. Look over there." She nodded toward the lake.

Phyllis looked in that direction and saw Jason Wilkes strolling beside the water, arm in arm with Teddy Demming.

"So he *didn't* fly back to L.A. after all," Melissa continued. "It doesn't look like he's making any secret of being with Teddy anymore, either."

"I don't see how that could have any bearing on the murder, though."

Melissa frowned in thought and after a moment said, "You know Lawrence made life miserable for Jason yesterday by humiliating him right out there in front of everybody. That's not the first time something like that has happened on this picture, although that was probably the most glaring example of it. If Teddy's in love with him — and look at her, she's gazing at him like she's a puppy! — she might've gotten so mad about Lawrence's treatment of him that she decided to get back at him."

"Maybe . . ." Phyllis said.

"And since Teddy's a production assistant — a glorified go-fer — people are used to seeing her scurrying around everywhere carrying things. If she took a piece of pie to Lawrence, nobody would think a thing of it. They'd probably forget all about it five seconds after they saw it."

Phyllis had to admit that Melissa's theory made sense . . . except for a couple of things. Murdering Lawrence Fremont seemed like an awfully extreme reaction to his dressing-down of Jason Wilkes. And like seemingly everyone else involved in this case, Teddy had no reason to dress the corpse like a scarecrow and lug it across the park to the log cabin. Teddy *might* have been able to do that, physically, Phyllis thought, but it would have been difficult.

Eve said, "Maybe she didn't intend to kill Fremont. She might have just meant to give him enough poison to make him sick and punish him for the way he's been treating Jason. His death could have been an accident."

Phyllis mulled that over and then nodded. "That seems plausible. One thing we haven't addressed in any of this speculation . . . Where did the killer get the cyanide? That's not something that anyone would just carry around."

"Whoever did it had to have gotten it ahead of time," Melissa said. "That means the poisoning was premeditated, whether the killer meant for it to be fatal or not."

Sam looked over at Ronnie and said, "Sorry you have to listen to all this gruesome stuff."

"Are you kidding?" the girl asked. "This is fascinating. And if I ever do become a cop, I'll have to deal with death all the time."

Carolyn said, "Not like this. Phyllis seems to attract it."

Phyllis had long since learned not to let Carolyn's comments like that bother her. She knew her old friend didn't mean any harm. Besides, whether she wanted to admit it or not, what Carolyn said had quite a bit of truth to it. She had been involved in far more murders than anyone in her position ought to be. Most retired American History teachers never solved even *one* murder.

"Premeditation rules out Teddy," Phyllis said, "at least as far as what Fremont did to Jason yesterday. If that had caused Teddy to go over the edge, she wouldn't have had a chance to lay her hands on cyanide here in the park." She waved a hand to take in their surroundings.

"Maybe, maybe not," Melissa said. "There's probably a maintenance shed around here somewhere that might have some insecticide in it, or something they spray on the plants, or who knows what else that might be poisonous."

"A spur of the moment thing, using what was at hand?" Phyllis mulled that over. "It seems unlikely to me, but I suppose we can't rule it out."

Melissa smiled. "See, I'm starting to think like a detective. I knew spending all this time around you would come in handy, Phyllis. Once we start shooting again, I'll be able to play you — I mean, Peggy Nelson — better than ever."

"Meanwhile, we've got a cherry pie to eat," Sam said. "I'm slicin' the rest of this sucker."

For the next few minutes, they concentrated on that, and the pie tasted as good as it looked.

"Could have used some homemade vanilla ice cream on it," Sam commented, "but cherry pie's hard to beat, ice cream or no ice cream. Of course, the same thing could be said of that pecan pie you baked, Phyllis. And I'm sure that spicy caramel apple pie would have been just as tasty. Lucky for all of us, pie isn't a zero-sum game."

"Oh, I know that from economics class," Ronnie said. "Just because *this* pie is good, it doesn't make any other pie less good."

"Right. When it comes to pie, they're *all* good."

Carolyn laughed and said, "Not all. I've been responsible for a few misfires in my time."

"Me, too," Phyllis said, smiling. "Anyone who has ever baked anything has had a few disasters along the way that they'd just as soon forget about."

Melissa said, "It's the same with movies. Lordy, I've made some that never show up anywhere except in the middle of the night on local digital channels desperate to fill up airtime. You can't even find 'em on You-Tube, and I'm glad of that."

Eve nibbled the last of the filling from her slice of pie, leaving a curving remnant of edge crust. As Phyllis watched her set that down on the paper plate, she thought about what Detective Largo had said earlier. The crime scene techs had found a piece of crust in Lawrence Fremont's motor home, the last link in the series of circumstantial evidence that they claimed pointed to Julie Cordell as the killer. Phyllis was pretty sure it wasn't possible to recover fingerprints from pie crust, but she wondered if they might be able to get any DNA from it. She knew from talking to Mike and other investigators in the past that such tests were a lot more difficult and time-consuming — not to mention usually less conclusive — than they were made out to be in movies and TV, but it might be worth talking to Isabel Largo again and making sure the police weren't overlooking anything.

Phyllis ate the last bite of her pie — including the crust — and started gathering up the plates and plasticware so they could go into one of the big trash cans scattered around the park.

"I'll help you with that," Ronnie volunteered.

Sam patted his stomach and said, "I think maybe I've had a mite too much to eat today. There was just so much good food, though, and I wanted to try all of it." He looked around. "They should've set aside part of the park and brought in a bunch of comfortable recliners so old guys like me could rent one of 'em and take a nap. That would've raised quite a bit of money, I'll betcha."

Carolyn said, "How could anyone possibly take a nap with all this hubbub going on?"

"Have you *met* Sam?" Eve asked.

He grinned. "Background noise makes for some of the best nappin'."

Phyllis and Ronnie dumped the trash they had gathered into a nearby can. "I need to go make a phone call," Phyllis said. "The rest of you go ahead and do whatever you'd like. I'll catch up to you in a little while."

"Is something wrong?" Carolyn asked.

"No, just something I need to check on," Phyllis said. She didn't mind sharing her ideas with the others, but in this case it was entirely possible Detective Largo would refuse to even speak with her, so there was no point in saying anything.

Sam started to get to his feet. "Be glad to help you, whatever it is," he offered.

Phyllis waved him back down and smiled. "Just sit there and digest your pie."

"I suppose I can handle that."

Phyllis walked across the park toward the parking lot, thinking it would be a little quieter up there. The crowd wasn't quite as big as it had been earlier in the day, and it would thin out more as the afternoon went on, but a lot of people were still there, talking, laughing, and generally having a good time. A certain level of noise went with that.

She stopped at the edge of the lot and got out her cell phone, which had Isabel Largo's number in it from a previous case. Phyllis called it, listened to it ring, and figured the call was probably going to go to voicemail. There was a good chance Largo wouldn't want to talk to her right now, after their brief and none too friendly encounter earlier in the day.

Then Phyllis frowned as she realized she was hearing the detective's phone ringing not only through *her* phone, but a ringtone was playing somewhere very close by, creating a rather discordant sound. She looked around and was surprised to see Isabel Largo getting out of a car parked a few spaces away. Phyllis thumbed her phone to end the call.

Largo walked over to her and said, "Whatever it is you want, Mrs. Newsom, we might as well do this in person since we're both right here. I saw you coming in this direction a minute ago and wondered if you were looking for me."

"I didn't even know you were here at the park anymore," Phyllis replied honestly.

Largo shrugged and said, "I thought I'd swing back by and see how things are going. The festival helps out a worthy cause." She nodded over her shoulder toward her car. "I brought a bag of canned food to donate."

"I'm glad to hear that. But the reason I was calling you is because I thought of a question I wanted to ask."

"Something else that's going to undermine the police department and its investigation?"

"That's just it," Phyllis said coolly. "You're not investigating anymore, are you? You've arrested Julie Cordell, so there's not any point in continuing."

"We're going to develop all the evidence we can," Largo snapped.

"Even if it clears Ms. Cordell, instead of strengthening the case against her?"

"We want to make sure we have the right person. We're just trying to get justice, that's all."

"Then we're working toward the same end," Phyllis said. "I was thinking about the pie crust you said you found in Lawrence Fremont's motor home."

She glanced toward the spot where the motor home had been parked the day before. Today a couple of pickups were parked there, their owners having come to attend the Harvest Festival. There was nothing to indicate that a murder had taken place in that spot.

"What about that pie crust?" Largo asked. "We already knew from the autopsy that Fremont ate cyanide-laced pecan pie. The evidence we found proves that Julie Cordell handled pecan pie. Finding the crust in the motor home just nails down the place where she gave it to Fremont."

"What about DNA?" Phyllis asked. "Is that piece of crust being tested?"

"To prove that Ms. Cordell handled it? That's actually not a bad idea." Largo paused. "That's why we sent it to the lab last night."

"Oh," Phyllis said. She tried not to feel too crestfallen. In the long run, it was good that Largo wasn't cutting corners. "What if the tests show that someone else handled the slice that Fremont ate, instead of Julie?"

"Then I'm sure your friend D'Angelo will be able to use that to Ms. Cordell's advantage. We should get the results back long before the case comes to trial. If they prove someone else is guilty, then I assume D'Angelo can get the charges against Ms. Cordell dropped."

"But in the meantime, Julie has to have

that cloud hanging over her head."

"That's the way the system works," Largo said.

Phyllis couldn't think of any argument to make against that statement. Like it or not, if she couldn't come up with anything to clear Julie's name sooner than that, they would have to wait for the results of the DNA test and hope for the best.

"Just out of curiosity, how big was the piece of crust they found?" she asked. "Was it a complete arc from the whole slice?"

"No," Largo said. She reached into her pocket, took out her phone, and swiped the screen a couple of times. Then she held it out so Phyllis could see the photo displayed on it. "That's it right there. It was only about an inch and a half long."

Phyllis looked at the segment of pie crust for a long moment and then nodded. "That appears to be from one of my pecan pies, all right," she said.

"And the one you brought was the only one in the park yesterday," Largo said. "That's pretty definitive, I'd say." She tucked the phone away. "Was there anything else you wanted to talk to me about, Mrs. Newsom?"

Phyllis shook her head. "No, I don't believe so. It just occurred to me to ask you about the DNA test." She managed a mile. "I'm glad you'd already thought of it."

Detective Largo nodded but looked like she didn't really believe the sentiment Phyllis had just expressed. "I'm going to walk around a little now."

"And I need to get back to my friends. Thank you, Detective."

"For what? I didn't help your case a bit."

"Well, you never know," Phyllis said.

CHAPTER 21

She found her friends at a display put up by the local quilting club, and the colorful quilts reminded Phyllis of her old friend Mattie Harris, who had been quite the quilter. That put her in mind of the Peach Festival held every summer in Weatherford and how one of those celebrations a number of years earlier had ended in tragedy. That was the first time she had been called on to solve a murder, and she never would have dreamed how things had gone since then. Not in the proverbial million years.

"These are gorgeous!" Melissa enthused over the quilts. "It must have taken ages to make some of them, they're so intricate."

"Quilting takes a considerable commitment of time," Carolyn said, "but it's very relaxing and also very satisfying when you're finished and you look at what you've created."

"I imagine so. I feel sort of the same way

when I watch a movie I'm in, although I don't ever really do that anymore. I haven't watched one all the way through in years."

"Why not?" Eve asked.

"Well . . . you wouldn't sit down and reread your book from start to finish just for fun, would you, now that it's been out for a while? You know all the stuff that went into it, and all the good and bad things that happened while you were writing it, and the magic just isn't there the same way it is for somebody who comes to it fresh. Basically, you'd rather read somebody else's book instead of the one you wrote. It's the same way with movies."

Eve nodded and said, "That makes sense, I suppose."

"Well, I figure on watchin' more of your movies, now that I know what to look for," Sam said.

Melissa laughed. "Oh, honey, just be careful! Like I said, there are some stinkers in there!"

Phyllis said, "I know they're going to finish making this movie with a new director, but what about any movies that Lawrence Fremont was supposed to direct in the future? I assume he had other projects in development."

"I'm sure he did, but the production

companies will just hire somebody else. It's possible that if a project is in the early stages, they might cancel it, but if there's a way to salvage things — and make money — Hollywood will find it."

Phyllis didn't doubt that.

"If I had more space, I'd buy one of these gorgeous quilts and take it home with me," Melissa went on.

"You could buy one and have it shipped to Los Angeles," Carolyn told her.

"I could, couldn't I? Which one do you think I should get?"

For the next several minutes, they looked over the quilts and discussed which one Melissa should buy. Phyllis took part in the conversation, but only distractedly. Her brain was still too full of the murder case, and her thoughts were whirling.

Once Melissa had made up her mind about the quilt, she approached the two older ladies who were running the booth and told them which one she wanted to buy. She offered the price written on the tag attached to the quilt, and one of the ladies said, "Don't you want to haggle a little first?"

Melissa laughed. "I'm not much of a haggler, honey. When I see something I want, I just go after it. Oh, and I'll need you to ship it to L.A. for me, too."

"Well, I suppose we can do that . . ."

The transaction was completed in a few minutes. The group moved on to see the rest of what there was to see in the park, although they were getting close to having seen it all. Around four o'clock, Carolyn said, "I don't know about the rest of you, but I'm getting tired. It's been a long day."

"Yes, it has," Phyllis agreed. "I think I'm ready to go home and rest."

"Sounds good to me," Sam said. "I'm not as young as I used to be."

Ronnie said, "Technically, I suppose I'm not, either, but I *am* still young. Is it all right if I stay here and some of my friends will bring me home later?"

"Would these be friends that I know?" Sam asked.

"Sure. Jennifer and Megan. You remember them from last year when you were a substitute teacher at the high school."

"Yeah, that sounds like it'll be all right."

"Thanks, Granddad."

As Ronnie hurried off into the crowd, Phyllis asked Sam, "Do you really remember who Jennifer and Megan are?"

"Well, not really," he admitted. "When it comes to teenage girls, they're *all* named Jennifer and Megan, aren't they?"

"Don't worry, I know who she means, and they're good kids."

Sam nodded. "I figured if it was anything to worry about, you'd speak up."

Phyllis turned to Melissa and asked, "Are you going back to the hotel?"

"Yes, I think so. I want to check on Julie and make sure she's doing all right. She said she was just going to sleep most of the day, since she didn't get much rest last night in jail."

"When you see her, tell her not to worry."

"I can tell her," Melissa said with a dubious shake of her head, "but I'm not sure she'll believe me." She smiled. "But with you digging into this case, Phyllis, I'm sure it's just a matter of time until you've nabbed that killer!"

After eating all they had during the day, no one was really in the mood for supper, so they skipped having an actual meal and everyone was free to fend for themselves. Phyllis wasn't the least bit hungry, so she headed for the computer instead of the kitchen.

She was curious about Lawrence Fremont's career, having become convinced that the key to the whole thing would be found there. Her research had delved into

265

his background already, but this time she concentrated on the movies and TV shows he had directed. She was glad Sam had told her about IMDb, because it was easy for her to use that website to track the course of Fremont's directorial career, right from the start.

She clicked on each of his projects and pulled up the complete cast and crew, then ran her eyes down the list of names, looking for familiar ones.

Not every murder had its roots in the past. Sometimes a killing took place almost immediately after whatever incident motivated it. But Phyllis was convinced that Lawrence Fremont's death was a result, at least indirectly, of something had happened years or even decades earlier. Usually, it took a long time to build up enough hate to end another person's life.

She didn't just pay attention to the actors but studied the various writers and producers who had worked with Fremont as well, and on through the lists of all the craft and technical members of the crew. She came across a number of well-known names, of course. Fremont had worked with the elite of Hollywood, including many award-winning actors and actresses.

Fairly early on in Phyllis's search, she

found Melissa's name with her photo next to it. That listing was on the page for the early feature where she had played a small supporting part. Phyllis didn't recall ever seeing the movie, so she scrolled down to the synopsis.

The movie was a domestic drama set in a small Kansas farming town. Melissa had played a schoolteacher. Something they had in common, Phyllis told herself with a faint smile. Melissa had been quite beautiful in those days, Phyllis saw when she checked out the gallery of photos from the movie. It wasn't surprising that she had caught Lawrence Fremont's eye.

Her curiosity satisfied, Phyllis clicked back to resume her investigation into Fremont's career. Julie Cordell had appeared in two or three of his pictures. Melissa's name showed up again in several other roles, as she had mentioned. Alan Sammons was listed as an associate producer on several features, then as producer or executive producer on others as his own power and influence in Hollywood grew. Jason Wilkes had written the screenplays for two of Fremont's films, both of them action/adventure movies. Those weren't collaborations with Deanne and, judging by the dates they had been made before she came to California and met and married Jason, Phyllis was a little surprised to see that Earl Thorpe had been either the first or second assistant director on nearly a dozen of Fremont's movies, dating back some fifteen years. Fremont must have liked working with Thorpe and had made sure he was part of the crew on those pictures.

And why wouldn't he like working with Thorpe, she asked herself, when it was clear that Thorpe was willing to do more than his share of the work and let Fremont take the credit for it?

A growing sense of frustration crept into Phyllis's mind as she clicked and scrolled, clicked and scrolled, through page after page of movie information, drawing steadily closer to the present day.

Eventually she found herself on the page for *Fresh Baked Death* and smiled as she saw Eve's name listed in the credits as the author of the source novel. No matter what else happened, nobody could ever take this bit of movie immortality away from Eve, and Phyllis was glad for her old friend. She scanned the cast and crew list, since she didn't know the names of most of the people involved in the production, only the ones who had come to dinner at her house a couple of nights earlier. Just like with

Fremont's earlier movies, she didn't find a thing that seemed like it might have any bearing on the case.

Maybe her hunch that she would find the motive for the murder in Lawrence Fremont's career was wrong. Some of her theories had been proven wrong in the past. In one especially tricky instance, she had been convinced three times that she had solved the case, only to have her theories collapse. Of course, in the end she had identified the real killer, but she was hardly infallible.

Fremont had another picture lined up to shoot next, Phyllis recalled. What was the title of it? She frowned as she tried to remember, and she had just come up with *The Bancroft Inheritance* when she realized that the website would have that information easily accessible at the click of a mouse. She didn't want to rely on the Internet for *everything,* though. Her brain still worked and could make connections that no computer could.

At least she hoped that was true. But as she studied the page that was already in place for Lawrence Fremont's next movie, she wasn't so sure. A number of the cast members were already lined up, and although Phyllis saw some familiar names, none of them were in this movie. The producer was different, and the script was by someone she had never heard of, based on a legal thriller novel she had never read, written by someone else she had never heard of. Talk about a dead end!

And yet, as Phyllis looked at the screen, her eyes narrowed. Something was there. She just wasn't seeing it. She looked down the list of cast members again. A handsome leading man and a beautiful leading lady, playing lawyers — and lovers — who wind up on opposite sides of a big case. A hulking criminal who admits to all his other misdeeds but steadfastly maintains his innocence in this case. A perky, pretty young paralegal who stumbles across the truth and finds herself targeted by killers. It didn't sound like a movie Phyllis would rush to watch, although it might be a decent enough way to spend a couple of idle hours.

So what in the world was it that struck her as being so familiar? She stared at the screen until her eyes ached, and it was there but remained frustratingly out of reach.

"What's that?" Sam asked from behind her.

She looked around and saw that he was holding a plate with a sandwich on it. The sandwich contained two thick slices of ham, plus cheese, lettuce, tomatoes, and pickles.

"Good grief," Phyllis said. "How can you be hungry enough to eat something like that?"

"Well, we've been home from the festival for a while," Sam said as if that explained everything. "A couple of hours, at least."

"Really? It's been that long?" Phyllis had been lost in her research and hadn't paid any attention to the time.

"Yep." Sam gestured toward the sandwich. "You want some? I'd be happy to go cut it in two."

"No, that's all right. I'm still not very hungry. I've been trying to figure out why Lawrence Fremont was murdered."

"You've got no shortage of suspects, that's for sure."

"That's why I've been concentrating on possible motives, instead."

"By looking up his old movies?"

"That's right. I was hoping I could spot some connection I hadn't found yet." Phyllis shook her head. "But no such luck. I feel like it's right in front of me and I just can't see it."

"You will," Sam told her. "You always do."

Phyllis smiled and said, "I appreciate the vote of confidence."

"That's one thing I've always got."

"That, and a big sandwich."

"Well . . . yeah," Sam said.

CHAPTER 22

Eventually, Phyllis gave up searching the Internet and put the question of motive out of her mind for the time being. Ronnie was late enough coming in that Sam got worried for a while, but then she showed up, apologizing for not letting him know that she had gone shopping with her friends after they left the festival. Sam accepted the apology but told her to text him next time she did something like that.

Later, after Ronnie had gone upstairs, he said to Phyllis, "You think she was tellin' the truth about goin' shoppin', or was she up to mischief somewhere, maybe with some boy?"

"I believe she was telling the truth, but it comes down to the fact that you either trust her or you don't."

"Oh, I trust her," Sam said. "But I also figure I'm a pretty trustworthy sort of fella myself, and when I was growin' up, I didn't always tell my folks the truth about where I was or what I was doin'. No teenager's a hundred per cent honest."

Phyllis said, "No child is ever a hundred per cent honest with a parent, no matter how old they are. I think it's just human nature to, well, shade the truth a little now and then. Just like it's human nature for a parent to always worry about a child, regardless of how old and responsible that child may be. Ronnie's your granddaughter, but right now you're acting as her parent, so you're going to be more concerned than normal."

"And she's gonna fib to me now and then."

Phyllis shrugged. "I'm afraid it's unavoidable. But for what it's worth, she's a good kid. I don't think she's going to deliberately get into a lot of trouble."

"I'll keep my fingers crossed," Sam said. "You want to watch a movie?"

"Do you think we could find that one Melissa made with Lawrence Fremont when she was young? The first one of his pictures she was in? I don't remember ever seeing it."

"We'll take a look," Sam said.

As it turned out, the whole movie wasn't available anywhere on-line, but there was a trailer for it on YouTube. Phyllis and Sam watched that, and Phyllis was struck again by how young and attractive Melissa was.

"You know, at this age she really reminds me of someone else," Phyllis commented.

"You?" Sam suggested.

"Oh, goodness no. I was never that pretty."

"We'll have to agree to disagree about that. I've seen plenty of pictures of you from back then, and you were 'way prettier. Still are, comes down to that."

"That's just your opinion."

"And I'm stickin' to it," he said.

They wound up watching a different movie directed by Lawrence Fremont from a few years earlier, the one with Robert Harkness in it that had prompted the clash between Harkness and Fremont. The picture was a drama set on a military base in the deep South during World War II. Harkness's Southern accent was a little shaky, Phyllis thought, with hints of his true Australian accent sneaking in now and then, as Melissa had mentioned, but Phyllis wondered if she just picked up on that because she was aware of the background. A regular viewer who didn't know any better might not have noticed a thing.

By the time the movie was over, Phyllis was ready to turn in. The last two days had been exhausting, and she was tired in both brain and body. She had learned some things today and theorized others, but the pieces didn't fit together to form a complete picture yet. She sensed that she was still missing something.

But maybe a good night's sleep would allow the answer she needed to bubble to the surface of her thoughts.

Or maybe it wouldn't, because when Phyllis woke up the next morning she knew she was still as far away from the truth as she had been when she went to bed the night before.

That was frustrating, but she wasn't going to let herself brood over it. The world had plenty of angst in it without that. Instead she went downstairs to the kitchen and started thinking about breakfast. She'd come across a new recipe for gluten-free pancakes that sounded like it might be good. Carolyn liked to avoid gluten for the most part because too much of it made her rheumatoid arthritis worse, although she risked it now and then, such as eating small slices of the pies Phyllis had made and the cherry pie Sam had bought at the festival the day before. Carolyn usually left some or all of the crust uneaten, though.

That wouldn't have helped Lawrence Fremont, since the deadly cyanide had been in the pecan pie filling.

Phyllis had the ingredients she needed for the pancakes, so she got to work on them. Carolyn came in a short time later, realized immediately what Phyllis was doing, and said, "How thoughtful. I appreciate you looking out for my health this way, Phyllis."

"That's what friends are for," Phyllis said. "And for getting the coffee started."

"I can certainly do that!"

It was Sunday and all of them were fairly regular church-goers, but Phyllis wasn't sure she felt up to it today. Not only was she still tired from walking around the park most of the day on Saturday, but the case was still weighing her down as well. She said, "I feel bad about it, but I may skip services this morning."

"I was just thinking the same thing," Carolyn admitted.

From the doorway between the hall and the kitchen, Sam said, "If there were any mountains close by, we could go out and do some worshippin' in God's natural church, like ol' Hipshot Percussion did in the comic strips."

"Goodness, I didn't know you were up," Phyllis said.

"I guess I sneaked up on you."

"And I probably haven't thought about Hipshot Percussion in forty years!"

Eve showed up in the kitchen a few minutes later. The pancakes were good, especially after Phyllis topped them with a little whipped cream and added some bacon on the side, the coffee was very good as always, and the company was excellent. It would be difficult to improve on her life, Phyllis mused as she sat at the table with her friends, or at least it would be if people would just stop getting murdered around her!

Everyone lazed around for the morning, and by the middle of the day Phyllis felt almost completely recovered from the strain of the past 72 hours. She and Carolyn prepared a light lunch using the leftovers. Sam had football to watch, and Phyllis was undecided whether to read or to try her hand at researching more of Lawrence Fremont's life. She already felt as if she knew the man better than she ever would have wanted to.

Before she could make up her mind, her phone rang and decided things for her.

"Hey, Phyllis, it's Melissa. I hope I didn't catch you at a bad time."

"No, not at all. We were just taking it easy today."

"I was wondering if maybe you'd meet me at the park in a little while. I've had some more thoughts about the case, and I want to take a look around the place while it's not full of people."

Phyllis glanced out the living room window. The day had turned rather blustery, with a thick gray overcast. This time of year, cold fronts blew through fairly often, and she could tell by looking at the way the mostly bare tree branches swayed that a chilly wind was blowing. Not only that, but she had wanted to get away from the case for the day, too.

On the other hand, she was curious what Melissa wanted to tell her. She asked, "You're not doing the last of that filming at the park today?"

"No, we're supposed to do that tomorrow. It's good that it worked out that way, too, because the weather isn't as nice and sunny today as it was on Friday and we need that to match, at least to a certain extent. The forecast says it'll be better tomorrow."

Phyllis thought for a second, then said, "I suppose I could go over there for a while."

"That's great. I'll meet you in, say, fifteen minutes?"

"I'll be there," Phyllis said.

Sam already had a football game on the TV, but he had muted the sound when Phyllis's phone rang. As she ended the connection with Melissa, she told him, "You didn't have to turn the sound off."

"The day I need some talkin' head to tell me what's goin' on in a game, that's the day I'll quit watchin' sports. I can follow along just fine on my own."

Since he had coached various sports for years during his teaching career, she knew he was right.

"Was that Melissa?" he asked.

"That's right. How did you know?"

"Just by the way you were talkin'. The two of you get along pretty well. Reckon that's because you're so much alike."

"I wouldn't say that," Phyllis responded. "But she asked me to meet her down at the park in a few minutes. She has some more ideas about Fremont's murder."

"That gal's just full of ideas."

"She is," Phyllis agreed. "She really seems to be enjoying playing detective."

"Want me to come with you?"

Phyllis thought about it for a moment, then said, "I hate to take you away from your game . . ."

"Oh, that's no problem," Sam said as he

got to his feet. He pulled his phone from his pocket and held it up. "I've got an app that keeps me up to date on everything that's goin' on in the game."

"Well, if you really don't mind, I'd be happy to have the company."

"Glad to do it. Want to take my pickup?"

Phyllis thought about it for a second, then said, "No, I'll drive this time."

She went upstairs and got a jacket thick enough to stand up to the wind. As she came out of her bedroom, she met Carolyn in the hall.

"Where are you going?"

"Down to the park to meet Melissa and talk about the case."

"Your new best friend," Carolyn said.

"Hardly. But I'm curious to know what she has to say."

"Well, I suppose it might turn out to be helpful, although it might not. When are they going back to Austin?"

"They're supposed to finish their shooting at the park tomorrow, weather permitting," Phyllis said. "I suppose they'll probably go back to Austin the day after that."

"Having those Hollywood people around has been . . . an interesting experience. I'm afraid I never could get used to such decadent lifestyles. I know someone who would fit right in out there, though."

Carolyn looked pointedly at the closed door of Eve's room.

"She's part of movie history now," Phyllis said, "and always will be. That's actually quite an accomplishment."

"I suppose."

Phyllis went on downstairs and out through the kitchen where Sam was waiting to the garage. On a Sunday afternoon, especially a blustery autumn Sunday during football season, Weatherford's streets weren't as busy as usual, although there was some traffic, of course. She made good time, and when she pulled into the parking lot, her Lincoln was the only vehicle in sight.

That didn't last long, though, because Melissa's rental car turned in just a few minutes later and came to a stop not far from the Lincoln.

As it did, Phyllis heard Sam's phone buzz. "Is that your football app?"

Sam took out the phone and checked the screen. "Yep. Looks like Dallas is tryin' to stage a comeback. I didn't expect *that* to happen."

Phyllis thought about the conversation she intended to have with Melissa and came to a decision.

"Why don't you just stay here and keep up with the game?" she suggested.

"You said you wanted some company."

"Yes, but how often do the Cowboys actually make a comeback these days?" She smiled to take any sting out of the words.

"All right, but roll the window down so that if you need me you can just holler."

Phyllis held the button down to lower the driver's side window and then got out of the Lincoln to meet Melissa.

The first thing Phyllis asked was, "How's Julie doing?"

"As well as can be expected, I suppose," Melissa replied with a shrug. "I talked to her yesterday evening after I got back to the hotel. Your lawyer friend Mr. D'Angelo had been there to see her, and I think that raised her spirits some. He strikes me as a fighter."

"He is," Phyllis said. "He does everything in his power to help his clients."

"I'm glad to hear that."

"Is there anything going on with the others in the group?"

"Well, Jason and Deanne are getting a divorce. I don't think *that* comes as a surprise to anybody. Deanne won't have any trouble moving on. Jason seems to think that what he's got with Teddy Demming is permanent, but I don't expect that to happen. Girls fall for those artistic types, you know, but it hardly ever lasts because they're such high maintenance."

Phyllis shook her head and said, "I wouldn't know anything about that. I've never been around an artistic type . . . other than Eve, of course."

"And none of her marriages lasted, did they? Don't I remember reading that she's been married several times?"

"That's true," Phyllis said. She didn't explain that various tragedies, including murder, had brought about the end of Eve's marriages. Her being artistic enough to write a novel hadn't had anything to do with it.

While they were talking, Phyllis and Melissa had been walking along one of the concrete paths toward the log cabin with the dogtrot where Lawrence Fremont's body had been found. When they reached it, Phyllis said, "You told me you had some new ideas about the murder . . ."

"That's right. I think I've figured out how Lawrence's body got down here." She pointed. "There's the answer to that, right there."

Melissa's finger was aimed at a portable toilet about twenty feet away.

Chapter 23

At least a dozen of the green portable toilets had been brought in for the festival, and the company that provided them wouldn't pick them up until Monday. Phyllis frowned as she looked at the one nearby that Melissa indicated.

"Are you saying that the body was hidden in the toilet first and then put in the dogtrot later?"

"No, I'm saying Lawrence walked into that thing —"

"With the scarecrow outfit in a bag or box or something," Phyllis broke in as the scenario abruptly came into focus in her mind. "He was still alive then, and he dressed himself as the scarecrow, walked out, and sat down in the dogtrot before the cyanide he consumed in the motor home had had time to kill him!"

"That's the way I figure it. Do you know why he did that?"

"He was going to play a practical joke on you and Julie. He thought he would wait until the camera was rolling and the two of you approached what you thought was a prop, and then he'd jump up and yell and scare you half to death. It would all be caught on film, too. That *was* the kind of prank he liked to pull, wasn't it?"

"It sure was. He'd waste half an hour of everybody's time like that, then chew somebody out if they delayed anything thirty seconds. He was a complicated guy. A real jerk, mostly, but a complicated one." Melissa shook her head and went on in an admiring tone, "You really figured out that scarecrow business in a hurry once it started to click, didn't you?"

"That's the way it tends to work with me," Phyllis admitted. "It's like finding the last piece of a jigsaw puzzle or pulling on one thread and having everything unravel."

"Those are opposite processes, but I get your meaning."

"It's like yesterday evening, when I was looking at things on-line about Lawrence Fremont and his films, and I saw *something* that seemed to me like it ought to explain everything about the entire case, but I never could quite put my finger on . . . what . . . it was . . ."

She stared at Melissa as her voice trailed off. Melissa frowned, cocked her head slightly to the side, and asked, "Phyllis, what's wrong?"

"Annie Richmond," Phyllis said.

Melissa's expression changed. Her puzzled frown went away, replaced by stony lines of determination.

"You've figured it out, haven't you?" she said.

"Oh, I knew yesterday you were the only one who could have killed Lawrence Fremont," Phyllis said as her heart started to pound. She could tell from the look in Melissa's eyes that there was no point in trying to lie. They understood each other too well, even though they had been acquainted for only a short time. She went on, "What I hadn't figured out until just now was *why* you killed him. Annie Richmond is your daughter, isn't she? I knew she reminded me of someone when I saw her picture and read that she'd been cast to play the young paralegal in *The Bancroft Inheritance,* but it never struck me who she looked like until now."

"She's my daughter, all right," Melissa admitted, "but she doesn't know it. I gave her up for adoption when she was born. Hardest thing I've ever done, but I figured she'd be better off."

"Why?" Phyllis asked, driven to understand, even under these potentially dangerous circumstances. She glanced toward the parking lot where Sam was waiting in the car. So close, but he had no way of knowing what was going on down here. "There were plenty of single mothers by then. An unmarried woman raising a child didn't have anywhere near the same sort of stigma it once did."

"Because I knew I couldn't be a good mom to her and keep building my career! I had a chance at a part in a picture that was going to film in Rome. I wanted that, and the next part, and the one after that . . ."

"So *you* were better off without a baby." Phyllis knew it was a cruel thing to say, but she wasn't that worried right now about sparing Melissa Keller's feelings.

"I did what I had to," Melissa snapped, "but when the time came, I *was* a good mom. I protected my daughter."

"By killing Lawrence Fremont."

"You've seen her! Pictures of her, anyway. You know Lawrence would have gone after her. She's young and ambitious, she would have given in. I couldn't allow even a chance of that happening —"

"Because Lawrence Fremont is her father," Phyllis said as the last of it clicked into place.

"I never told him," Melissa said. "Not that he would have given a damn if I did. Lawrence never cared about anybody but himself. Don't you get it, Phyllis? He *deserved* to die. Not just for what he might do to Annie, but for all the terrible things he's already done. The way he's treated people over the years. He just wasn't a good man."

"That doesn't mean you can get away with killing him."

"I think it does," Melissa said, and she took a gun out of her jacket pocket.

Phyllis had known she was coming to the park to meet with a killer. That was why she had accepted Sam's offer to come with her. But she'd never intended to reveal that knowledge to Melissa. The sudden realization that the actress whose picture she had seen on-line was really Melissa's daughter had surprised it out of her. But even then, even knowing that the secret was out, she hadn't been terribly afraid of Melissa. Melissa had poisoned Fremont and gone about it in an elaborate way. Phyllis certainly didn't plan to eat anything Melissa might offer her.

Now it seemed that Melissa was willing to resort to more direct methods of accomplishing her goals, too.

"You can't shoot me," Phyllis said as she tried not to stare at the small, black, semi-automatic pistol.

"I don't want to," Melissa said. "I don't suppose you'd give me your word you'll never say anything about this?"

"I can't do that. And I can't believe you'd let a good friend like Julie be sent to prison for something you did."

Melissa made a face. "That was never part of the plan. I figured with as many suspects as there would be, as many people as Lawrence had harmed or just rubbed the wrong way, the police would never solve his murder. I never expected them to try to pin it on Julie, and for sure not this fast." She shrugged. "But the DNA evidence will clear her. They won't be able to prove she ever actually handled the slice of pie the poison was in, because she didn't, and I've seen enough of Jimmy D'Angelo already to know that he'll be able to sell the jury on reasonable doubt. Julie won't go to prison."

"But her name won't actually be cleared, either, so she'll always have that shadow of suspicion hanging over her." Phyllis paused. "Unless the DNA evidence is going to convict *you*."

"Don't hold your breath waiting for that,"

Melissa snapped. "I was careful when I —"
She stopped short.

"When you took the last slice of pie from
my house Friday night?" Phyllis asked.
"That's what you started to say, isn't it?
What did you do, wrap it up in some plastic
wrap you found in the cabinet, or something
like that?"

"How in the world do you *know* that? You
said you solved the case yesterday. How?
How could you have known any of it?"

"Pie crust," Phyllis said. "The edges of
the one I brought here yesterday were
crimped differently than the one I baked for
our dinner Friday. All that pie was eaten
except for one slice . . . that *you* offered to
take into the kitchen for me. Then later
when I saw it was gone, I figured you must
have given in to temptation and eaten it
after all."

"I gave into temptation, all right. As soon
as I saw how much Lawrence liked it, I realized I could slip him the poison that way.
I'm still not sure how you figured it out,
though."

"Fremont left a little piece of the crust,"
Phyllis explained. "Detective Largo showed
me a picture of it yesterday. As soon as I
saw it and realized it came from the pie I
baked Friday, I knew you were the only one

who could have taken it and used it as a murder weapon. And now I know why you did it. But the business about the scarecrow and the practical joke . . . that still baffles me."

"Phyllis Newsom, the brilliant detective! The crime-busting grandma! And I fooled you, didn't I" Melissa laughed, but it wasn't a particularly pleasant sound. "I knew if I was going to get away with it, I'd really have to muddy the waters. That's why I suggested the joke to Lawrence. I knew he'd think it was funny. I was *in on it,* you see. He thought he was just going to scare Julie. So he ate the pie when I brought it to him. He was looking over the script and was so distracted he never even noticed anything different about it. Then he took the scarecrow outfit in a bag, like you said, and changed over there in the portable toilet, and then it just took him a second to walk into the dogtrot and sit down. *That* was when the cyanide hit him." She shook her head. "I wish I could have been there to see the expression on his face."

The wheels of Phyllis's brain were still turning. She said, "After that, you volunteered to 'help' me solve the case, but only so you could keep feeding me different suspects, like Earl Thorpe and Teddy Demming and Mr. Sammons. You thought you'd keep me off-balance that way and make sure I never figured out what really happened. It worked, too."

"But only for forty-eight hours," Melissa said with a shake of her head. "Actually just twenty-four, since you said you knew yesterday I killed him. Damn, Phyllis, you really are as good as your reputation. I believed I could outwit you, though. I told you, I studied you. I know how to get into the characters I play. I figured I could make Peggy Nelson just as good or better than Phyllis Newsom."

Phyllis realized then that Melissa wasn't completely right in the head. She said, "This is just a game to you."

"No. Not a game. Not where my daughter is concerned. But the rest of it . . . recreating that earlier murder, matching wits with you, running rings around the cops . . . I've got to admit, it was a pretty good acting exercise."

"You fooled me into thinking you were actually a decent human being," Phyllis said. She didn't even try to keep the note of bitterness out of her voice.

"That's why they call it acting," Melissa said coldly as she lifted the gun a little more. "Now walk on down to the lake."

Phyllis was scared, no doubt about it, but she wasn't going to cooperate with a killer. People who tried to do that almost always wound up dead themselves. Instead she asked, "What are you going to do?"

"It's a real shame, but after I leave here, you're going to fall in that lake and drown. A tragedy that will keep Lawrence's murder from ever being solved. I know I can't trust you to keep our little secret."

"I'm not going to just let you drown me."

"They say it's an easy way to die. Easier than cyanide, anyway. But I *will* shoot you if I have to."

"People know I was meeting you here." She didn't say anything about Sam being in the car. Maybe Melissa hadn't noticed him . . . Maybe he would look this way and see the gun . . .

Phyllis's heart sank a little when she realized that she and Melissa had moved around enough that the corner of the cabin obstructed most of the view from the parking lot. Sam might notice what was going on, but there was a better chance that he wouldn't.

"And maybe I'll be a suspect. But it's more likely the cops will think somebody came along and robbed and killed you. After all . . ." Melissa smiled. "You and I are friends, right? I'd never hurt you. And there won't be anybody smart enough to see the truth —"

A rush of footsteps came from the dogtrot behind them. Melissa started to turn, but before she could, a burly figure slammed into her from behind with enough force to send her flying off her feet. The pistol sailed out of her hand as she crashed heavily to the ground.

Phyllis moved fast, running to where the gun landed and snatching it up. She held it in both hands and pointed it at Melissa. She expected to see Sam, coming to help her as he had numerous times in the past, but instead it was Earl Thorpe who loomed over the fallen actress, breathing hard from exertion and probably emotion, too.

"Do you want me to . . . take the gun . . . Mrs. Newsom?" he asked.

"I've got it," Phyllis said. "You should call 911, Mr. Thorpe, and then you should tell me what you're doing here." She smiled faintly. "Although I'm very glad that you showed up when you did."

CHAPTER 24

"Deus ex machina," Eve said.

"What?" Carolyn asked.

"It translates from the Latin as 'god from the machine', but it's actually a literary term for the plot technique where some unforeseen character or incident pops up at the end to totally change things. Some people regard it as a cheat, but I'm not sure it actually is, because goodness, things that we don't foresee happen all the time in real life, don't they? And if art is going to properly reflect reality, then such things could occur sometimes in fiction, too, couldn't they?"

The five of them — Phyllis, Sam, Carolyn, Eve, and Ronnie — were sitting in the living room Sunday evening, after Phyllis had spent several hours being questioned by Detective Isabel Largo and Chief Ralph Whitmire. The district attorney had shown up fairly late in the conversation, and after being filled in, he had assured Phyllis that first thing Monday morning, he would file a motion to have all charges against Julie Cordell dismissed. He'd practically been gritting his teeth when he said it, but after looking at the video Earl Thorpe had recorded on his phone from where he was hiding just around the corner of the dogtrot, there hadn't been any other choice.

"Well, Earl had a good reason for being there," Phyllis said in response to Eve's comment. "He was around on the other side of the lake figuring out how to set up some shots from that perspective when the filming started again. He saw Melissa and me, even though we never noticed him, and came around the lake to talk to us. But then he saw her pointing the gun at me and heard what she was saying, and luckily he had the presence of mind to record the rest of the conversation."

"And the bulk to bowl her over and knock the gun out of her hand," Carolyn said.

"Yes, that certainly was lucky for me."

"What gets me," Sam said, "is how I never even noticed what was goin' on, all because I was payin' attention to some danged old football score."

"You couldn't have known. *I* didn't know what was going to happen. I didn't plan on letting her know that I'd figured it out. That was just an unfortunate slip on my part, possibly because I'd been so frustrated about not being able to pin down what was bothering me. I know now it was the resemblance between Melissa and this Annie Richmond."

"Who's nowhere near Weatherford and never has been, as far as we know," Eve pointed out. "That's why I said it reminded me of a *deus ex machina*. That's not necessarily a bad thing. I mean, the ancient Greeks used it all the time in their plays, and those are classics."

Carolyn said, "Yes, because they're full of murder and perversion and appeal to people's baser instincts."

"What are they gonna do about the movie now?" Sam asked. "I can see how they might be able to replace the director, but Melissa's the star and she's locked up."

"And half crazy, to boot," Carolyn added with a snort.

"I imagine they'll have to cancel it, or at least postpone production for a while," Phyllis said. "They're bound to have some footage without Melissa in it that they could use if they recast her part." She looked over at Eve. "Does this affect how much you get paid?"

"Not really, at least not yet. I've already

been paid for the rights. I'm supposed to get a tiny percentage of the profits, but from what I've been told, the studios and the production companies have such creative accounting departments that technically it'll never make much of a profit, if any. So that's not really a consideration. However . . ."

Eve smiled.

"What is it now?" Carolyn asked suspiciously.

"I've talked to Mr. Sammons, and you're right, Phyllis, they do have enough non-Melissa footage in the can that it's worth trying to salvage. He's going to pitch the studio executives on the idea of turning the whole thing into a cable TV series instead of a movie. He really liked the suggestion I made about how to improve it, too."

"And what suggestion would *that* be?" Carolyn wanted to know.

"I told him they should put some zombies in it!"

AUTHOR'S NOTE

Holland Lake Park in Weatherford actually exists, but as in the earlier novel *The Pumpkin Muffin Murder,* I've taken considerable liberties with its geography. This version of the park is more like it exists in my memories of the days my husband and I took our daughters there to play when they were little. The Harvest Festival is completely fictional, as are all the characters and events in this novel.

■ ■ ■ ■

RECIPES

■ ■ ■ ■

PHYLLIS'S OLD FASHION PECAN PIE

Ingredients
3 tablespoons brown sugar
1 cup granulated sugar
1/2 cup dark corn syrup
1/2 cup light corn syrup
1/4 cup butter
4 eggs
1 teaspoon vanilla
1 1/2 cups pecans, (half coarsely broken
   and half pecan halves)
1 unbaked deep-dish pie shell

Directions
Preheat oven to 350°F (177 degrees C).

In saucepan boil brown and granulated sugar and the corn syrup together for 2 to 3 minutes. Add butter to the hot mixture and set the pot aside letting the butter melt and the mixture cool slightly.

In large bowl beat eggs lightly and very slowly pour the syrup/butter mixture into the eggs, stirring constantly.

Stir in vanilla and pecans and pour into crust. Turn over any pecan halves that are upside down. Cover crust with a strip of aluminum wrap to keep from browning too much.

Bake for about 45 to 60 minutes or until set.

TEXAS BRISKET

Ingredients
1 tablespoon meat tenderizer
2 tablespoons chili powder
1 tablespoons salt
2 teaspoons ground black pepper
1 tablespoon garlic powder
1 tablespoon onion powder
1 tablespoon sugar
2 teaspoons dry mustard
1 bay leaf, crushed
4-6 pounds beef brisket, trimmed
1 1/2 cups beef stock
1 tablespoon liquid smoke
2 tablespoons Worcestershire sauce

Directions
Preheat the oven to 350 degrees F (177 degrees C).

In a small bowl combine tenderizer, chili powder, salt, black pepper, garlic and onion powders, sugar, dry mustard, and bay leaf to make a dry rub. Season the raw brisket on both sides with the rub. Place in a roasting pan and roast, uncovered, for 1 hour.

Add beef stock, liquid smoke and Worcestershire sauce, and enough water to yield about 1/2 inch of liquid in the roasting pan. Lower oven to 300 degrees F (149 degrees C), cover pan tightly and continue cooking for 3-4 hours, or until fork-tender.

Trim the fat and slice meat thinly across the grain.

HOMEMADE FLOUR TORTILLAS

Ingredients
2 cups all-purpose flour
1 teaspoon baking powder
1/2 teaspoon salt
1 tablespoon lard
3/4 cup water

Directions
In a large mixing bowl mix the flour, baking powder, and salt together. Mix in the lard with your fingers until the flour resembles cornmeal. Add the water and mix until the dough comes together; place on a lightly floured surface and knead a few minutes until smooth and elastic. Divide the dough into 12 equal pieces and roll each piece into a ball. Let the 12 balls rest under a damp cloth for 10-20 minutes.

Preheat a large skillet over medium-high heat. Use a well-floured rolling pin to roll a small dough ball into a thin, round tortilla. Place into the hot skillet, and cook until bubbly and golden; flip and continue cooking until golden on the other side. Place the cooked tortilla in a tortilla warmer; continue rolling and cooking the remaining dough.

Makes 12 tortillas

RANCH STYLE BEANS

Ingredients

16 ounces of dried pinto beans
pinch baking soda
1 teaspoon olive oil
6 cloves of garlic, minced
1 onion, diced
1 15 ounce can of tomatoes (or 2 medium-sized tomatoes, peeled)
1 4.5 ounce can mild, chopped green chiles
2 tablespoons chili powder
1 teaspoon brown sugar
1 teaspoon apple cider vinegar
1 teaspoon paprika
1 teaspoon cumin
1/2 teaspoon oregano
1 cup of water
6 cups of beef broth
Salt and black pepper to taste

Directions

Rinse the dried beans thoroughly. Add a pinch of baking soda to help with digestion issues. Soak them covered in water — either overnight or the quick soak method in which you place the beans in a pot, cover with water, bring to a boil, cover and remove from heat and let sit for one to two hours.

Drain the soaked beans and rinse.

In the pot you'll be cooking your beans, heat up a teaspoon of olive oil and cook the onions for ten minutes on medium. Add the garlic and cook for another minute. Throw the cooked onions and garlic in a blender and add the tomatoes, green chiles, chili powder, brown sugar, apple cider vinegar, paprika, cumin, oregano and a cup of water. Puree until smooth.

Add the pinto beans and beef broth to the pot and stir in the chile puree. On high, bring the pot to a boil and then cover; turn the heat down to low and simmer for two and a half hours, stirring occasionally. Check beans for tenderness. Cooking time can be as short as two and a half hours and as long as four hours. When you're satisfied that the beans are done, salt and pepper to taste.

TEXAS CAVIAR

Ingredients

3 green onions, chopped
1 orange bell pepper, chopped
2 jalapeno peppers, chopped
1 pint cherry tomatoes, quartered
1 cup frozen corn thawed
1 (15 ounce) can black beans, drained
1 (15 ounce) can black-eyed peas, drained
1 (0.7 ounce) packet Italian dressing mix
1 tablespoon avocado oil

Directions

In a large bowl, mix together green onion, bell pepper, jalapeno pepper, cherry tomatoes, corn, black beans, black-eyed peas, Italian dressing mix, and avocado oil. Cover and chill in the refrigerator approximately 2 hours.

Spinach Pomegranate Salad

Ingredients
juice of one lemon
2 tablespoons honey
1 (10 ounce) bag baby spinach leaves,
  rinsed and drained
1/4 red onion, sliced very thin
1/2 cup roasted pecans
1/2 cup crumbled feta
1 pomegranate, peeled and seeds separated

Directions
In small bowl mix the lemon juice and honey until blended. Place spinach in a salad bowl. Top with red onion, pecans, and feta. Sprinkle pomegranate seeds over the top including any juice, and drizzle with lemon honey mixture.

VERY VEGGIE POTATO OMELET

Ingredients
1/4 cup each: sliced mushrooms, sweet onion, bell pepper, fresh spinach, and diced tomato
3 tablespoons olive oil
1 large russet potato peeled and shredded (grate on the big holes of a cheese grater)
4 large eggs
1/4 cup water
Shredded cheese for topping

Directions
In a medium skillet, sauté the mushrooms, sweet onion, and bell pepper until desired texture. Turn off the heat and add the tomato and spinach. Cover with a lid until ready to use.

Preheat large skillet on medium. Add potatoes in an even layer in the pan, and cook until golden crisp on the bottom.

Mix the eggs and water in a bowl while potatoes are cooking.

Flip the potatoes over in the skillet. Add the egg mixture on top of the potatoes. Cover with a lid for a couple minutes to get the eggs to solidify some. Check the eggs. If still too wet in the middle, use your spatula to work the egg down into the potatoes a little. While the middle is still a little wet, add the precooked veggies (the spinach and tomato will have steam wilted, but not become gooey).

Fold in half and top with cheese and season with salt and pepper to taste.

SPICY CARAMEL APPLE PIE

Crust

Ingredients
3 cups pastry flour
1 teaspoon salt
1/2 cup shortening
1/2 cup cold butter
1/2 cup ice cold water
1 tablespoon white vinegar

Directions
Sift the flour and salt into a large bowl. Cut in the shortening and the butter until the mixture resembles coarse crumbs. Mix the water and vinegar together in a cup. Add the mixture to the crumbs. Mix together just until the dough is combined and handles well.

This recipe makes enough for a double crusted pie.

Filling

Ingredients
6 tablespoons salted butter
1/2 cup white sugar
1/2 cup brown sugar

1/4 cup water
1/4 teaspoon cinnamon
6 apples, peeled, cored and sliced
2 tablespoons grated ginger
3 tablespoons flour
1 pastry for double-crust pie

Directions
Preheat oven to 425 degrees F (220 degrees C).

Combine butter, white sugar, brown sugar, water, and cinnamon, in a saucepan over medium heat. Bring to a boil, remove from heat and set aside.

Roll out half the pastry to fit a deep-dish 9-inch pie plate. Place bottom crust in pie plate.

Toss apple slices and ginger in flour, then place on the bottom crust in an even layer.

Roll out top crust an inch larger than the pan. Cut into 8 (1-inch) wide strips with a sharp paring knife or you can use a pizza wheel. Weave the pastry strips, one at a time, into a lattice pattern. Fold the ends of the lattice strips under the edge of the bottom crust and crimp to seal.

Pour butter-sugar mixture over top of pie, coating the lattice, and allowing any remaining sauce to drizzle through the crust.

Bake in the preheated oven for 15 minutes. Reduce heat to 350 degrees F (177 degrees C), and bake until the crust is golden brown, the caramel on the top crust is set, and the apple filling is bubbling, 35 to 40 more minutes. Allow to cool completely before slicing.

GLUTEN-FREE OAT NUT PANCAKES

Ingredients
1 1/2 cups rolled oats
1 1/4 cups mashed banana (about 2 very
   large bananas)
1/4 cup plus 2 tablespoons low fat sour
   cream
1/4 cup plus 1 tablespoon nonfat milk (or
   substitute milk of choice)
3 large eggs
2 tablespoons maple syrup
1 1/2 teaspoons baking powder
3/4 teaspoon ground cinnamon
1/2 teaspoon kosher salt
1/2 teaspoon ground nutmeg
1/2 cup chopped walnuts or pecans

Directions
Place the oats in the bottom of a blender.
Process a few times to grind, then add the
mashed banana, sour cream, milk, eggs,
maple syrup, baking powder, cinnamon,
salt, and nutmeg. Blend on high speed, stopping to stir a few times as needed, until the
batter is very smooth and well combined,
about 2 minutes. Stir in the chopped nuts.
Let sit 10 minutes.

Heat a griddle or a large, well-oiled skillet

over medium high heat. Spoon batter onto skillet and cook until bubbles begin to form. Flip, and continue cooking until golden brown on bottom. Repeat with the remaining batter Serve immediately with toppings of your choice.

ABOUT THE AUTHOR

Livia J. Washburn has been a professional writer for more than thirty years. She received the Private Eye Writers of America Award and the American Mystery Award for her first mystery, *Wild Night,* written under the name L. J. Washburn, and she was nominated for a Spur Award by the Western Writers of America for a novel written with her husband, James Reasoner. Her short stories "Panhandle Freight" and "Widelooping a Christmas Cowboy" were nominated for a Peacemaker Award by the Western Fictioneers, and her story "Charlie's Pie" won. She lives with her husband in a small Texas town, where she is constantly experimenting with new recipes. Her two grown daughters are both teachers in her hometown, and she is very proud of them.

CPSIA information can be obtained
at www.ICGtesting.com
Printed in the USA
FFHW020748220319
51198536-56673FF